CAN'T QUIT YOU

T.K. RICHARDS

AUTHOR'S NOTE

Stream the single, "Can't Quit You" on all music platforms. https://distrokid.com/hyperfollow/noahgrove/cant-quit-you-special-version

This novel contains mature content, mentions alcohol, and slang of a Southern dialect. For example, a character may speak using words such as bouta, which means about to, or gonna, which means going to. Other words are cut off to reflect the manner in which the characters speak, such as beaut to reflect beauty. Characters switch with clarity during dialect. Maeva is sometimes called Maev for short. Michelle is called Chelle.

<u>Name pronunciations</u>
Maeva (May-vah)
Nya (Nie-yah)
Souse (S + house - the h)

"They don't know about our love."

—JON B.

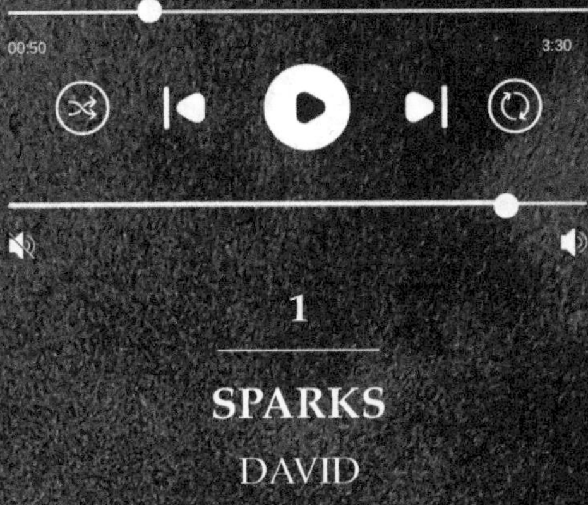

1

SPARKS
DAVID

SONG: "SPARKS" BY COLDPLAY

"Slow night, boys. You're on in five." Honest John taps the wood near the curtain.

I open my mouth to bargain for fifteen with hopes the seats near the stage will fill when she blows in like the wind. Her wild, curly hair bounces as a breeze of fresh air blows through the club entrance door behind her.

Short beige nails remove the strands falling into her eyes. That's when they hit me. I swallow hard when her hazel-brown orbs glisten in the top lights. Her lashes bat away as she looks around the dive. Everyone is staring at her. Especially me. How can I not? She's breathtaking, literally stealing the air I breathe from a few feet away.

I've never seen her 'round these parts before. Sure, a few pretty girls show off their legs in cut-off shorts from time to time to give the locals something to get excited about. But all the ass shaking and exposed limbs in the world can't compare to the entrance of this *beaut* gracing us tonight—gracing *me* with her presence. And certainly not in this dive.

Her unfamiliarity doesn't stop me from watching her strut to the bar with her hands tucked inside the back pockets of tight blue jeans with holes ripped at the thigh. A white tank accentuates her top curves stacked in the most glorious of places. Upright and round. Her tan skin highlights in the grooves under the fluorescents: pink, green, blue, and red they turn. Below them, she is luminous. Stunning. A smoke show. And definitely not from 'round these parts.

I stalk her every move from the crack in the curtain until she glances my way. I turn my head toward Moe, my big brother and drummer of the band, yapping his gums.

"Don't fight me on this, David." He points then pokes my chest.

I nod as if I'm listening to him rant about how he wants tonight's show to kick off. Having not heard a word he said, I agree. The guys grow silent as this is against the norm.

"What's with him?" Lim, our bassist and keys man, also first cousin, asks.

Moe shuffles my hair. "Yeah, what's with you? You normally give me grief."

The guys give me a hard time but sound muffled, as if I'm under water. I haven't a clue what they're saying and fan them off, listening to my heart pound in my ears. All I want to do is look at her. All I *can do* is look at her.

I lower my head so they don't catch me staring in her direction. Subtly, I take peeks of her conversing with the bartender. With his arms spread wide, he faces her, finally cracking a grin as he grabs a tall glass from below the bar.

She watches him carefully as he mixes her order, then he slides it to her on a napkin and throws up his hands. She sips through a straw. Her lips are divine in action. Supple, wet, and easy. She smiles for the first time since strolling in this dump. I wonder, *Why would a woman like her have a reason not to smile? The whole world should be worshipping her, bowed at her feet. And I with them. Maybe I will one day, if she'll allow me the honor.*

Honest John calls us to the stage. Before he steps on, he pays us half of our fee since the crowd is scarce.

"If the place picks up its numbers by the end of your set, I'll give you the other half. Have a good show." He walks off before we argue with him, confident we won't cancel our performance with the few coins he's placed in our hands.

The guys don't put up a fuss since we're using the place as practice for a big audition at the end of the month.

"Well, boys, we've got gas money for the van." Souse, our lead guitarist, jokes then stuffs the bills in his pocket.

"Gotta crawl before you walk," Moe reminds us. "And we'll be running soon."

I look out at the audience. The regular drunks at tables 5 and 6, the two midweek bartenders, a tip-hungry waitress, and Honest John carry on, not at all excited about our set. Then my eyes set on *her.*

Even with her back to me, I feel her magic. Nerves I haven't felt in years tingle my veins as I follow Lim onstage. One of the drunk dames gives us shit and screams, "It's about damn time!"

Lim signals her a thumbs up and sits at his keyboards. Souse follows with Moe on his heels, and I greet the small crowd.

"How's everybody doing tonight?"

The ladies at table 5 hoot and raise their beers.

"We're Zone 615. Thanks for rockin' with us tonight."

The men at table 6 tell us to fuck off with their glares and turn up their lips. We tune our instruments with a few quick runs of notes to amp up the crowd, waiting for Moe to tap his sticks together for us to begin.

My eyes turn to the lovely creature sitting at the bar. I examine her exquisite frame. Her perfect back and silk-clad shoulders tease me under the frozen solid blue light above her head. She is distracting. Everything about her essence I find hypnotizing.

I nearly miss Moe starting the set the way he said he would with slow-paced beats on the drum as Lim blends a heavy bassline in. I adjust my straps on my shoulder one final time as my toes tap to the rhythm, and I step to the mic and release my first note of the night.

"Tell the boss man to shove it where the sun don't shine, tell your boyfriend it's over and you are now mine."

The lyrics of stealing another man's woman work like a charm on rowdy bunches that hang out in dives like *The Murf*. Every eye in the house shifts to the stage, hungry for the next line.

Souse bursts in with a guitar chord to speed up the pace. I take a breath and deliver the next line, belting my heart out, when the *beaut* swings around in her chair.

My chest pumps with adrenaline from performing but also from the way her hair ripples across her shoulder when she spins to look my way. Her beauty stifles me, and my voice fights through hell not to crack.

To hold my focus, I look away from the bar, catching up with the lyrics a millisecond late. With my eyes fixated on the cords draped in front of me on the edge of the stage, I collect myself then shift my eyes over to Souse sensing something's off with me.

He touts his lips and questions me with raised brows. I nod to him discreetly, averting my eyes to the corner. As they guide him to the bar, he glances her way, then back to me, shakes his head and smiles. His reaction forces me to grin alongside him.

Sometime during my exchange with Souse, the vixen made her way to the dance floor just below the stage. The grin is wiped away from my lips as I feel a second choking sensation rise in my throat.

Right in front of me, she glows like a firefly, weakening me at the knees, oblivious of her power to potentially ruin our set with her enchanting spell swirling all around me. Her hips sway to the beat of the drum while her lips tease me, sipping from the half empty glass in her hand.

She licks her lips, and my zipper tightens.

Control yourself, David. Calm down, boy.

While I try to convince the rush of blood shooting in my pants to take a U-turn, the catalyst is doing nothing to warrant such a reaction except existing, clueless of her effect as I struggle not to lose control.

I turn around to look at the boys sharing glares at me behind my back, but like a magnet, my eyes wander back to her rocking hips compelling me.

Our eyes meet as I sing the bridge of the song, and sweat drips from my hair down the sides of my face.

Are the lights too bright tonight? I wonder, aware the heat I feel isn't coming from the lights. It's her, warming my body like summer nights in the south.

My pulse races as I try to break our gaze. I fail as our eyes lock. I stare into hers from above, defeated in the battle of her beauty holding my attention. I'm done. Over. Succumbed by something electric.

Her perfect body moves to the music. Her big hair swings side to side past her shoulders. Her breasts jiggle above the top hemline of her tank. Her soul reaches for mine.

Nervously, I mouth the chorus line, unsure that I'm saying the right lyrics and in turn singing what's going on in my mind to the now alert standing crowd.

I want her. Can she tell? Are we having a moment, or is this all in my head?

Singing lead in a band, I tend to fancy myself as the most wanted by the groupies, so I'm careful with who—*and how* I engage with women in places like this. But this encounter feels different. Authentic. Surreal.

Electricity from my guitar enters my fingers and transcends

like waves into her body. My eyes appear to deceive me as I see flashes surround her. I question if anyone else bears witness to us connecting and become fixated on the orange light in a cigarette, which reminds me of the joint I smoked in the van. I shake off the illusion, but then, currents and sparks flow between me and this girl, and we bond.

I feel alive, like a charged energy has found me, and look to the band for support, but they're ignorant to what is happening to me on the inside. They tease me with goofy looks and wagging tongues from their mouths, unaware I've been struck in the moment.

I exhale and finish off the song Moe picked, which turned out to be the best choice, and imagine the laughs we're gonna share after the show, while butterflies flutter in my stomach and my cheeks turn to blush while a goddess awakens me on the deepest level—a level I didn't know exists.

Helplessly, I gaze upon her when the song ends. She stands still, lost in my world as we speak with our eyes, then smiles at me. My spine tingles as my voice sounds loud in my head, and she breaks my stage persona, getting me to smile back at her.

Oh yeah, baby. It's go time.

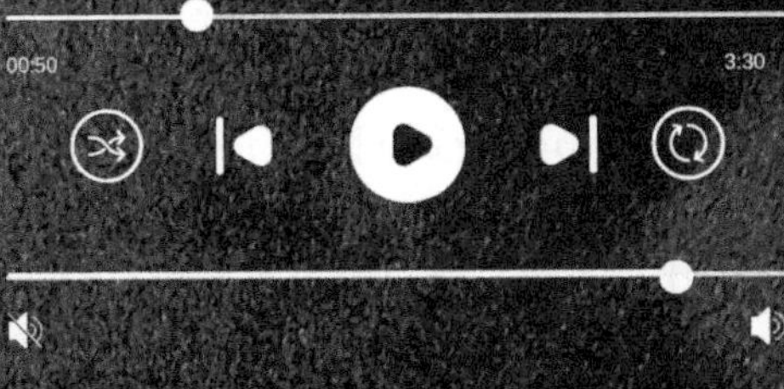

2

———

WHEN YOU WATCH ME

MAEVA

Song: "When You Watch Me" by Poppy Ajudha

Mom pops out of her bedroom like a bat out of hell when I grab my keys from the counter.

"Maeva! I'm not fussing."

My head rolls up to face the ceiling.

"This isn't our stomping grounds. I'd prefer you roam around when the sun is out."

"I won't go too far, Ma. I promise."

She sighs. "Be careful. And don't come in this house too late. It's late enough as is," she preaches.

I give her the usual nod.

God I can't wait to be on my own. As soon as Pop gets better, I'm blowing this country town.

I drive the speed limit, culture-shocked at the vast difference between Murfreesboro versus Charleston, the only home I've ever known.

The roads are black and empty. I shake my head, being the only person out this time of night.

"A few months of this life in the sticks, and I'm outta here," I say to myself, channel-surfing the local radio stations for a plug.

My friends back home think I'm crazy for taking a gap year after we graduated last summer. But I made the choice to stay behind and help take care of my Pop, and now this move to Tennessee.

For the life of me, I wish Ma hadn't transferred jobs, which brought us here. Staying home to be the good daughter my parents needed while still being near the water made putting RIT in upstate New York worth it. But out here, with no beach, no friends, and no night life, is cruel and unfair. It's no way to spend yet a second summer of my stalled introduction to adulthood.

Nashville isn't too far away from this town, but my mother chose a house far past the outskirts—Murfreesboro, TN.

Just my luck.

The full moon lights the streets while I explore. I hear Ma in my head saying, "The quiet will be good for a change."

"It's definitely quiet. And dead as a doornail," I mutter below a country song. "This summer is going to suck," I add, still talking to myself as the radio station plays a double play of the woman singing the hell out of a song about a truck. "I need to add this lady to my playlist."

For miles and miles, her voice keeps me alert in the darkness. It doesn't look like there's much to get into 'round these parts. All I see are dirt, and dirt roads, green pastures I imagine are filled with cows, and mom-and-pop shops.

Everything is closed as I drive a little longer in the vast, open, quaint town where retirement would be nice—away from the noise, wildlings, and city life.

Finally, a few lights appear ahead, and my shoulders sting with excitement. A Waffle House sits on the corner. Across from it, a gas station and a Wendy's. To the left, an abandoned building occupies a lot next to a hair salon and laundromat, and on the right of it, an automated car wash next to a used car lot with royal-blue, yellow, and red triangle banners flying above the steal barricade to its entrance.

I travel a little farther down the road and pull into a gravel-filled lot of a dimly lit bar with blue and red lights flashing above the doors. A *Come On In* sign with an illustrated, blonde-haired, white lady wearing skanky red pumps and a blue crop top holds a beer in her hands.

I lock my car door and make my way inside with a twenty-dollar bill in my front pocket and fake ID in the right one just in case I'm carded. Judging by how sketchy the place looks, I assume I will be able to get a drink with no problem.

"Thank God they have AC," I mutter under my breath, halfway hanging inside the dingy door.

The heat still blazes late at night, something the town has in common with back home, minus the humidity. Still, it only takes a second to dampen my skin during the quick hop and a skip I make to get inside the shithole.

My instincts tell me to turn around and go home once I see the hole-in-the-wall bar is a rundown mess, but the cool air blowing on me from the loud unit above my head feels too good to leave so fast.

I talk myself into enjoying one drink and grab a stool at the nearly empty bar. The bartender looks up at me then returns to drying glasses at the other end. I raise my finger.

He moseys down at his leisure. "What can I do you for?"

"What's your specialty?" I smile at him.

He returns my smile with a furrowed brow and grins. "You're not from 'round these parts. Are ya?" A grunt follows his question.

I look him in the eye. "That obvious, huh?"

"To me and everybody else in here."

I spin around on the stool and notice several eyes are upon me. Sitting at faded Jacobean tables and chairs, close to six women stare at me. They look angry. The rest of the people just look like they've made the same bad call as I have—spending their free time in the grungy dive.

"Everyone?" I scoff. "Ha! This place is damn near empty."

"That may be, but I see what your back can't."

His eyes shift to the right while his mouth grins at me on the side. I follow his leading gesture to a flimsy black curtain off to my left. Brown shoes and white sneakers are visible at the foot of the drape, and an eye stares at me through the opening, but the face is obscured.

I turn back to the bartender and make my second play. "I didn't catch your name."

"I never gave it." He smirks.

"Then, I'll call you friend. So, friend, about that drink?"

"Oh God, spare me. I've got a charmer on my hands." He scoffs. "You got some sort of ID on you, gal?" he asks, drying another glass with the towel attached to his apron.

I lift my ass from the stool, reach inside my pocket, then hand him my fake ID. His brows furrow, so I lean forward on the bar to study his skepticism of the card.

He laughs and flicks it with his finger. "Between you and me, I know this is a fake. It's a good fake, though, so I'll give you something light if you got the cash."

I reach in my other pocket and flash the twenty-dollar bill.

"How old are you, really?"

I boldly lie, "Twenty."

The bartender sighs. "So, more like eighteen."

He catches me with my mouth open. I hesitate to correct him, and he chuckles.

"Nineteen last month," I admit.

"You better not get me fired, *youngin'*. Something light coming right up."

He taps on the chestnut-coated wood and places one of the glasses he's cleaned on the counter.

I press my luck, teasing him with a slick comment. "Easy on the juice."

He pauses, shakes his head, then walks toward the mini-fridge in the center of the bar station. I wiggle my fingers at him with a curve on my lip, watching him drown my glass with soda water.

He places the glass on a square napkin. "One mojito for the young lady. That'll be six dollars."

I scowl at him. "Six dollars for a glass of soda water? Come on, man. You didn't even garnish it with mint or a piece of fruit. Do you even have fruit back there?"

We share an awkward silence.

"I'll give you five bucks."

He rests his hand on his side of the bar. "Five bucks, you drink it, and get out of here before you get me in trouble."

"Deal. Got change for a twenty?"

A grunt vibrates from his throat. "Tell you what. This one is on me. Hurry up, sip and get out of here."

His tone offends me, yet I apologize for being a nuisance and slip the twenty-dollar bill back into my pocket.

"Sorry..." I wait for him to give me his name.

He stares at me with both brows raised now.

"I didn't come in here to make an enemy. Just need to take the edge off."

He sticks out his chest. "Says everyone in here." He huffs. "You don't belong in a place like this anyhow. Go home and gossip with your friends on the phone or something."

Over our banter session, I raise my glass and give him a salute. "Thanks for the drink."

The rum soothes my throat with warm flavors found in the islands. I swirl the libation around with the straw then get lost in my thoughts, appreciative for my first few moments of alone time in days.

The music over the speakers lowers as a band tunes their

equipment on the stage. I sip from the glass fast, with plans to leave as the bartender ordered, then raise it to catch his attention, hoping he'll come take my money and make me a stronger blend.

A male voice appears over the speakers. "How's everybody doing tonight?"

I mock him while laughing to myself.

Everybody? There's no one in here.

The bartender returns and removes the empty glass in front of me. Slowly, I slide the twenty-dollar bill over to him.

"Fix me a real drink, please, and keep the change for your trouble."

His shoulders slump as he reaches for a fresh glass. "You're cut off after this one."

Quickly, he mixes me another mojito then places the cash in the tip jar. Onstage, the drums start off slow, and the music from the radio fades into the background once the bass player kicks off a rhythm. I close my eyes and listen to the band come together with a snazzy melody as the flavors of the mojito, mixed stronger this time, burst in my mouth.

I take another swig and savor the flavor. Mid-swallow, I give the bartender a thumbs up, opening my eyes when the voice of a legend speaks to me. A mixture of soul, grit, and power with a sexy and edgy rasp of fragility woos me. It's a voice to shame all other voices. A voice too good to be singing in a shithole bar in the middle of nowhere.

The strings of the guitar add a liveliness to the song, and the rhythm increases on the count. I stop sipping on my cocktail and sit still as the night, waiting for the singer to send another chill down my spine.

The voice returns to sing the next line. I swivel on the stool and turn toward the stage. My body shivers. The low, country, soulful register make the hairs on my arms stand up. I'm fully drawn to this man's voice fluttering waves in my chest.

My body itches to take a closer look, so I float to the stage to observe the songster with a critic's eye. I watch him up close as he croons into the mic. I judge him. He's not the man of my dreams at first glance but cute enough to sing me into submission.

Each verse he sings makes me feel like I was meant to stumble into this very bar, just to hear him sing. And I listen with open ears and an open heart.

From afar, he appears shy, staring at the floor as he hits every note with perfection. His full head of dirty-blond and brown hair looks dry under the stage lights, and the day-old scruff on his face adds to his appeal. But my God, his voice. I have never heard anything like it. It captivates me so much I give him a pass for those busted brown Sperry loafers on his feet.

Normally, a fashion faux pas of that magnitude turns me off. But something about him and his voice helps me overlook his bad choice of footwear tapping on the dusty stage floor.

Whatever magic his angelic voice is working on me piques my interest when he looks up and stares into my eyes. He sings to me. Yes, me. I can't prove it, but I know it. I'm sure of it. I feel it.

We share a moment and speak to each other from a distance in a language of our own. His lips. My heart. Our eyes. Our souls.

His voice puts me in a trance, creating fairy tales in my mind of him kissing me under the moonlight, singing me to sleep, and playing tunes next to a fireplace. Scenarios I never pictured before but wish would come true.

I freeze in my stance from the unknown encapsulating me. My back falls weak from an intrusive current, and I shiver. An energy bursts inside my veins so compelling that I open my mouth and exhale the rush of wind trapped in my chest.

For a second, I think it's the music seeping in my bones. But I'm wrong. It's him.

My eyes hold his attention, and he blushes while serenading me, gazing at me from the stage. Making love to me with his words and his voice. Unifying our worlds with music.

This isn't what I planned to find in a place like this. Nor is it the good time I was searching for. But I'll take it.

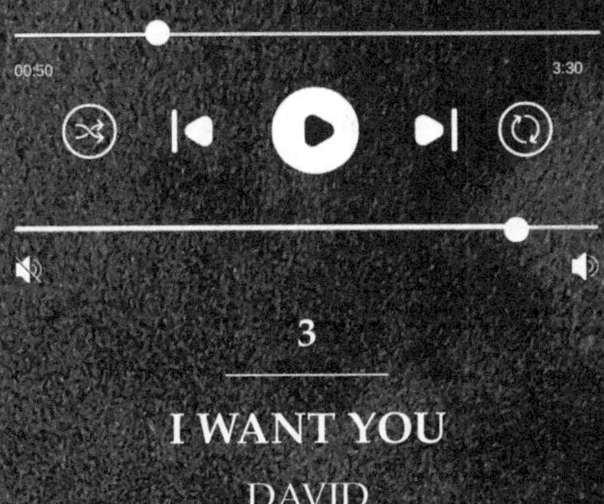

3

I WANT YOU

DAVID

The guys give me pure hell once we finish our set. Moe grabs me from behind and places me in a headlock while the band takes turns giving me nuggies. I softly punch his stomach and fight my way out of Moe's hold, strong-arming him like when we were kids.

"Alright. Alright. Take it easy, will ya." I raise my fists, ready to trade blows.

"What was that in the opening?" Moe teases. "I've never seen you sweat so much, bro."

"And I've never seen you move that fast to pack up the equipment," Souse adds.

No lies are being told between us. I did hurry to break everything down with one eye on my mystery girl. Her gleaming eyes screamed she wanted to get to know me, just as bad as I needed to know her, and nothing was gonna get in the way of that happening.

I flip off the guys and peep my head into the audience from the side of the stage. A sharp pain strikes my chest.

She's gone.

I exit stage left and race over to the bar. Vince, the bartender, throws a lime on a customer's bottle and offers me a beer on the house.

"No thanks." I look over my shoulders.

"Let me guess. You're looking for that fiery filly?" Vince grins.

I lower my head to hide the smile taking over my entire face and nod. "Give me something, Vince. Who is she?"

"New girl in town. Pretty young, though. The name on her ID ain't the real one, I can tell you that much. Seems to have a decent sense of humor, though."

"Damn." I drop my head. "I missed my shot." The news erases the rosy rush of red beaming on my cheeks and wipes away the goofy smile on my lips. "You think she'll come back?" My voice reeks of desperation.

"Pretty sure of it." His eyes travel behind me.

A light breeze of soft flowers hits my face to the right. The beauty sits in the stool next to me, pretty as a penny, and smelling like the perfume section in a department store.

I swallow deep and choke on my words. "Hey," I manage to get out with a jittery voice.

"Hey." She puckers her lips.

Her whiskey eyes hold mine like before. They're prettier up close as I stare into them, and captivate me until her supple nude lips press together. I daydream what it would feel like to taste them until her chuckle breaks my gaze.

"I was hoping to catch your name. I'm David by the way."

Her face emits a golden radiance of light as she blushes. "David. I guessed you'd have more of a rock star name, like Solo or Razor." She studies me for a brief second. "I'm Maeva."

"Maeva. Pretty name for a pretty girl. I might change my name to Razor. How'd you come up with that?"

"Your voice is razor sharp."

"Is that right?" The goofy smile returns, and I feel like a moron. "Did you like the show?"

"Loved it—a lot, actually." She tucks her bottom lip under her teeth.

I pause, pleased at how our conversation is flowing, mesmerized by the way her skin and eyes blend of perfection, enamored by the sexy way she moves her mouth.

"Cool. Cool." My words drag until I snap out of my daze. "What'd you like about it?"

Maeva looks up into my eyes. "The singer."

My face turns redder than clay on a softball field.

She continues, "He's got an amazing voice. Made me feel like I was being serenaded."

I turn away and catch Vince smirking at me while pretending to clean beer mugs, then I clear my throat and collect myself.

"Where are you from?"

She props up in her chair. "Charleston."

"It's nice there. What brings you to Tennessee?"

"Family."

"You plan on staying 'round these parts long?"

Please say yes. Please say yes.

"'Til the end of summer." She smiles. "I'm heading off to college in the fall. Are *you* planning on staying around here long?"

My eyes gaze deeper into hers. "I plan on following you around."

She laughs at my horrible pickup line. I join her in laughter, even though I'm dead serious. My heart skips at the sound of her voice expressing joy and the way her amaretto skin beams at the height of her cheeks.

"Can I buy you a drink?" I ask her.

Her laugh disappears, and her demeanor turns cold. She looks up at Vince giving her a stern eye then back to me.

"I better not. I promised the warden over there I wouldn't get him fired."

Vince nods.

"Well, how about this... Any chance you'd join me at a party tonight? A few friends of mine are having a bonfire out at the corn maze. I'd love to talk with you some more."

"A corn maze? Bonfire? In this heat?" She scoffs. "I'm definitely not in the city anymore."

"*Nawl,* baby. You're in the good ol' country now." I beat my chest.

Her shoulders shrink as she covers her mouth with her hand, masking a giggle. She straightens up her form and turns to me with a serious face.

"I'll give this corn maze thing a try if you promise to, one, not kill me; two, not let anyone else kill me; and three, not keep me out too late."

Silence creeps in between us, and I lean against the bar like a lame dick with no sense of humor.

"David, I'm teasing. But...not really about the first two."

Slower than molasses, I catch on to her joke.

So, she's funny too.

"I guess that joke didn't go over well with you, huh?" She parts her lips and raises her brow.

"I'm gonna be honest with you. I'm cussing myself out for not catchin' on sooner." I pluck my head, feeling like an idiot. "For a second there, I was afraid you were serious." I chortle and hide my face below the shade of my palm. "Scout's honor to follow rules one through three. Say you'll come—at least for a little while."

4

KISS ME

DAVID

*M*aeva takes a long pause after I beg her to hang out, eyeing me from head to toe. Tension forms in my shoulders, and I panic I've come on too strong, too soon, and blew it.

She looks down at her phone, then raises her eyes to meet mine. "I'll follow you out there. But if it doesn't feel right, I'm out," she states, clear and firm.

"Cool. I'm gonna go tell the guys it's time to get up outta here. Be right back."

I rejoin the band hanging out near the back exit. The vibe is stale when I walk up. After being met with ridicule and judgmental stares, I open my mouth to apologize for not helping load the van.

Souse cuts me off. "Thanks for all your help, Loverboy."

I hold up my hands. "Guys. I'll make it up to you. I promise."

"We're just joshing." Moe scruffs my hair. "She's hotter than The Fourth, so all is forgiven."

I gloat. "She agreed to come to the bonfire tonight."

"Speaking of which, we better get a move on before the gate closes."

I hightail it back to Maeva and follow her to her car.

"Nice wheels," I say, running my hands over the hood of her bumblebee-colored Camaro.

She presses the button on her keyring and swings her big, wavy hair over her shoulder. "Graduation gift. Last year." She clicks her tongue.

The door unlocks, and I open it for her.

"*What'dya* say I ride with you, and we follow the band over to the field?"

"Hop in." She stops me with one foot in the car. "And no funny business, or I'll whip this baby and fling you out on the side of the road like in the movie."

"Yes, ma'am." I snicker under my breath. "I'm a fan of *Transformers* also."

"Let me guess, Megatron?"

"How did you know?"

"All the cool guys root for the villain."

She thinks I'm cool.

The guys almost catch me cheesing like a Cheshire cat as they pull in front of Maeva's car. She flashes her headlights, and we follow them for a short drive to the maze.

The car is quiet for too long. I'm still tripping that she described me as cool, and I don't know how to respond. Afraid we're quickly losing the chemistry we had at the bar, I turn on the radio.

She side-eyes me. "That was quick."

"I'm sorry?"

"You... Running out of things to say."

My mind musters up topics I think will impress her to get the mojo between us going again. I think to mention how clear and black the sky is and how the stars are shining bright alongside the full moon. Instead, I settle on talking about her, being that she drives sensibly with her hands at the ten and two positions on the wheel.

"Seems like I could trust you with my life. Do you always drive this careful, or is it because you have a passenger aboard?" I ask behind a grin.

Her tongue clicks, and she smiles. "I could drive for Nascar if I wanted to," she brags.

Her pretty lips pucker. I tuck my fingers below my legs to refrain from touching them.

"Nascar? Ha. So, you do have a little country in you."

My joke breaks the ice. The awkward vibe lifts, and the pucker on her lips transforms into a grin and a humorous scowl above her brows.

"That's what he said," she mutters.

I partly hide my face with my fingers. She continues to boast about her driving skills and schools me about the bells and whistles on her car. I watch her light up, spilling her knowledge on makes and models, telling me she's good with her hands in so many words.

We arrive to the grounds, and Maeva parks the car off to the side, by ourselves, in the lot. The band goes inside without us, yelling from the gate.

"You're cutting it close, D! Come on!"

Maeva turns off the engine and looks at me. "Should we talk about what happened when you were onstage?"

"I was hoping that wasn't all in my head." My voice deepens. "First time I've ever felt anything like it."

She sinks her teeth into her bottom lip. Our eyes meet, and I fall victim to the urge of doing what I wanted to do since the moment she walked into my world. I ease over the gear shift and gaze deep into her brown eyes. She closes them, and our lips touch.

The softness of her mauve lips compels me. A gentle, simple peck entices me to want more. I take a big risk and slip my wet, thirsty tongue in her mouth, overcome in the moment by her essence and sweet breath. Her rosemary-mint-scented hair and floral-infused perfume travels up my nose, imprinting her claim on me.

She's more intoxicating than the beers I had before my set.

She frees herself from my hunger and wipes her lips. "Your friends said we were cutting it close."

"Yeah. We should probably go inside."

I hop out, open her car door, and escort her to meet the group gathered around the fire. I introduce her, clenching my fists and threatening a select few of my compadres staring at her too long through a narrowed lens.

Maeva sits next to me for most of the night. She's quiet, babysitting a beer in her hand while the lot of us share stories of our high school days and old talent shows. The reminiscing creates requests for me to sing an old country classic we loved back then.

Moe runs to the van and grabs my guitar. Maeva snuggles closer to me as my friends grow rowdy with impatience, like entitled fans demanding a free performance.

"One song, and one song only," I say, tuning my strings for the proper key.

The circle mumbles when they recognize the melody of the song coming together. The unruly bunch hoots and hollers when I sing the first few words of the hit "The Gambler" by Kenny Rogers.

By the end of my solo, everyone around the fire is singing along, except for Maeva.

"One more!" they shout.

I whisper in Maeva's ear, "You get a special request."

Her forehead scrunches, and her cheeks blush. "Surprise me."

I smile at her for a second then announce, "I'll sing one more. This one's for Maeva."

Ooh and ahh moans from my friends cause me to laugh. I regain my composure midway and croon, *'The world was on...'*

Maeva's cheeks turn bright red in the reflection of the fire. I exhale, happy to know she's familiar with the classic hit "Wicked Game."

Thank you for this one, Chris Isaak.

Her knee touches mine, and that electric charge sizzles through my body again. Twice in one night convinces me our destinies align. I finish the tune, looking into her eyes, ignoring the cheers from the gang watching us fall for each other. Their cheers and carrying on sound like distant clatter below my heart pounding in my ears.

"Let's go for a walk." I take her hand and pass my strings to Moe.

We flee the party and find a vacant spot a quarter of the way into the maze.

"Am I the only one trippin', or is something happenin' here?" I wave my finger between us.

"You sang to me. It was beautiful." Maeva's body twists. "And no, you're not trippin'. I feel it too."

I still her jittery body by interlacing my fingers with hers. "What do you propose we do about it?"

"We have the rest of the summer to answer that question."

I can't control the impulse I have to kiss her again. I slide us further inside a pocket of bushes past the third curve and taste her whole mouth. My hands let go of hers, and my arms wrap around her back, holding her steady and close, where our hearts stretch to collide with every beat.

She tilts her head opposite mine, and our tongues linger in delight. Our noses meet, and we come up for air.

"It's getting late," she gasps and pulls away. "I should get home."

Selfishly, I retort and place my hands around hers. "Stay a little longer. I don't want you to go."

"I didn't intend on being out this late. I'm sure my mother is up worrying about me."

I struggle to let go of her hand and whine like a spoiled kid not used to not having his way. "When can I see you again?"

She hesitates. "Whatd'ya have in mind?"

"I'm up for anything as long as you say yes."

She checks the time on her phone. "We can work something out, I'm sure."

"You know the guys can find a way home. I can show you how to get out of here and follow you. You know, to make sure you get there safely."

Her voice wavers as she snickers. "I'm a big girl. I think I can manage."

She denies me one more time but allows me to walk her to her car. The guys follow us out and wait for me by the van.

Maeva stands against the door. I reach for her hand to take her phone. She jumps, and I grunt.

"You shocked me." She laughs.

"That was all you. May I?"

She places it in my hand, and I enter my number into her contacts. "Are you sure you can find your way out?"

She nods.

I stand aside and watch as the dust mists from under the rocks as she drives away. Once the red brake lights fade in the distance, I return to the gang whispering about me.

Souse nudges my arm. "We're going to meet so many fine birds when we go on the road, D. Now is not the time to get sweet on a girl. Keep your head in the game and your eye on the prize."

"And what if she is the prize?"

Moe places his hand on my shoulder. "Oh shit. I think my little brother is in love."

My brother is right.

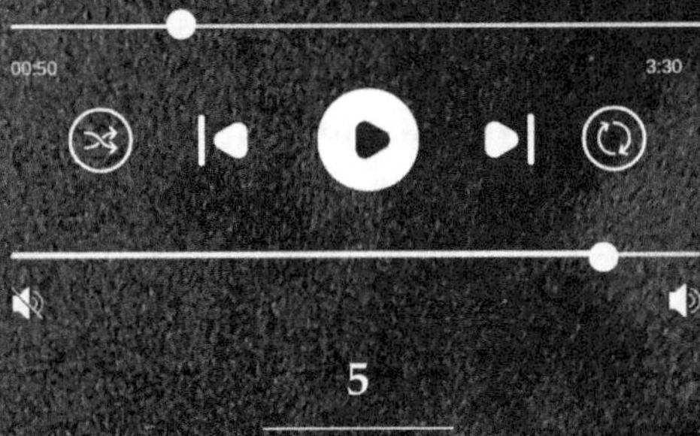

5

CRAZY FOR YOU

MAEVA

I leave the bonfire, surprised that meeting David's friends went better than I expected, minus the one girl ogling me with daggers all night.

My heart bleeds fear and confusion from the emotions I feel on the drive home. I question if the night was real or a figment of my imagination. I was serenaded by a vocal god, shared kisses with him in under an hour, and my body hasn't stopped tingling since his eyes held mine. Those glistening, oceanic eyes put images in my head that would shame the devil.

His mesmerizing voice travels with me home, affecting me in ways I've never known. I shake my head at my decision to trust him, follow him around a foreign town I could have easily gotten turned around in, and for kissing a stranger like that under the starry night sky without knowing anything about him.

Thinking of those kisses warms me all the way home, lasting with me and leading me safely out of the maze.

Is this what love feels like?

The porch light turns on when I shut off the engine. As

expected, Ma is waiting up for me. Her dark eyes greet me as she folds a throw blanket at the end of the sofa.

"You didn't have to wait up for me." I kiss her cheek.

"I told you not to stay out too long. We know nothing about these parts or these people. The neighbors have yet to come and say hello."

I grit through my teeth. "I don't think people do that anymore."

"What's with you?" Ma deflects when she refuses to be wrong. She changes the subject when any topic of discussion isn't leaning her way. "I saw you smiling in the car."

I was. And I couldn't stop.

I grin and lie through my teeth. "I wasn't smiling."

"You're doing it right now. Did I say something to amuse you?"

I hug her tight and mirror her tactic. "Good night, Ma," I say, skipping down the hall.

❤

THE LYRICS, *'I don't want to fall in love,'* carve on my brain like a permanent marker. I cue up the song on my streaming service and compare David's voice to the man singing the original while lying across my bed.

My bias prefers David's voice and acoustic version over the classic, but I replay it over and over throughout the night, cuffing my bud while thinking of the sexy scruff outlining David's full lips and chin.

I squeeze my thighs tight, giddy with the song playing on repeat, and crash out on a natural high sometime in the night.

Last night is fresh on my mind when I wake to a bird chirping and tapping on the gutters above my window. The song has been shut off, but last night's smile is still tattooed on my face when my mother walks in.

"Your father is still asleep. Breakfast is on the stove. And I see you're still smiling. Should I be worried?"

I cover my face with a pillow.

"We'll talk about this later on tonight." She clears her throat. "And turn that radio off when you're getting ready to go to sleep."

"It's not a radio, Ma!" I yell, muffled below the suffocating silk pillowcase.

"Have a good day!"

"You too, Ma!"

Time stands still all morning. I plan to call David sometime past noon, so the hours tease me, slowly rolling by. Filled with angst, I get Pop up for a walk.

"Let's get some sun."

The saying *'Make a plan and watch God laugh'* was exactly how I felt when I learned my parents needed me to put college off for a year. I was eager to be out in the world, all on my own, claiming my place as an adult. But if I had to make the choice to give up that dream again, I would do it in a heartbeat for my Pop.

I wheel his chair to his liking. Nice, slow, and careful over bumps in the road. His condition took some getting used to. He was always Superman in my eyes. So, when the car accident immobilized him, it devastated our family and changed the best laid plans I had set for myself.

We tour the layout of the new neighborhood, talking to each other with grunts and sighs at the yardwork, green grass, and all the state, rebel, and country flags swinging from the terraces.

"Ma was talking about how the neighbors haven't welcomed us. If they ever do and bring food, we probably shouldn't eat it."

"You saw that house, too, huh?"

"It's like you taught me. There's no escaping it. It's everywhere."

"And that's a sad truth."

We reach the front of our development. Children play in the

swimming pool and practice tennis on four courts. On the side of the clubhouse, the elderly exercise on the lawn.

Pop taps my hand. "I'd like to watch this session if you don't mind."

I sit next to him on a bench near the swing sets, hating he has to watch others do the things he is ready to do again.

"Think they'll let me join?" he asks.

"Pop, remember the doctor said not to rush your recovery."

"I'm getting tired of sitting in the house. I miss having a home PT. Have you and your mother made any calls yet?"

"We have, but in the meantime, you're stuck with me." I tap his hand. "Is that a problem? *You no likey* me anymore?" I pout my lips.

Pop chuckles. "You've been all smiles today. Who's the guy?"

"Dad," my voice drags. "How early does Ma get up to gossip about me?"

"The question is did she sleep at all? She looked exactly the way you do now when we first met. I recognize the glow. The light in your eyes, Pudding Pop." He chuckles.

An elongated sigh leaves my mouth. My cheeks turn rosy, and my heartbeat increases as I confess.

"I met someone last night while out on a drive. A singer. And if he's as nice as I think he is, I'll invite him over one day."

"Is it wise to get wrapped up with someone when you're leaving in how many weeks?" Pop raises a brow.

"Five weeks and three days."

"Don't let him or anyone else get in the way of your dreams— including me."

I squeeze my Pop's hand. "Being here with you is worth postponing school."

"This too shall pass. One day, you'll return from wherever, and your old man will be back on his feet. Now go sign me up for this woman's class." He points toward the elders stretched out on the lawn.

Pop taps out after I make him a sandwich and fries for lunch. With the house nice and quiet, I call David. The sound of women in the background puzzles me when he picks up.

"Maeva," he answers.

I hesitate. "Hi, am I interrupting?"

"Uh, no, not at all. I'm over my parents' house—talking about you, actually," he stammers. "Would you like to come over for dinner tonight?"

I place the phone to my chest until I hear his voice vibrate on the line.

"If it's too soon, I understand." His voice lowers, "I've been gloating about you all morning, so my family wants to meet you."

I sit speechless, clueless of the best way to respond without appearing silly or too eager to jump at the chance of seeing him again.

Meet his family?

"You there?" His voice awakens me from the conversation I'm having with myself.

I swallow the air trapped in my throat. "I'd love to. Send over the details."

I can sense David is smiling when I accept his invitation to dinner. But for a few seconds, I worry. Should I have played hard to get? Should I have said no? Will he think I'm easy? Then, I remember what my dad said earlier.

Am I getting too close to this guy too soon?

Anticipation of the evening overwhelms me as I try on a few dresses and play with my curls.

"Up or down?" I ask Ma, walking into the disaster zone known formally as my bedroom.

"I thought we were going to discuss you coming home late last night with that same goofy smile on your face?" She scowls at my outfit. "Where are you off to now?"

"I have a date. What's wrong with this dress?"

"It's too revealing. Wear the lilac one."

Since I'm meeting David's parents, I follow the advice from mine. I slip into Ma's choice as she stands in my doorway, expressing her doubt.

"Maeva, we've been in town for roughly a week. I'm not sure I like you going out on dates so soon. Your father and I haven't even met this boy."

"I have a feeling you will soon. I'm meeting him for dinner at his parents' house tonight."

"Isn't that a little fast?"

Pop leans his head in my room and winks at me. "Leave the girl alone, Marva. Let the young people have their fun and fall in love."

"Love?" Ma's voice rises to fuss. "Who mentioned anything about love? For God's sake, Louis, she met this boy less than twenty-four hours ago."

I finish sprucing my hair, adjust my dress at the waist, and take one final twirl in the mirror.

"Here's the address of where I'll be so you can stop worrying." I kiss both of my parents on the cheek. "I'll let you two have your lovers quarrel now. Don't wait up."

"Don't wait up?" Ma warns, "You better not come home at the devil's hour."

I dash to my car and plug in the address. Twenty minutes later, I arrive at David's parents' house.

"Turn around and call him to cancel," I say to myself, convinced I don't belong.

The gated community intimidates me. My neighborhood is nice—slightly above middle class. David's side of town screams *we are in the one percent.* Private lake, six tennis courts, two massive pools with slides and a cascading waterfall at the entrance, smooth, black tar roads, and bricked in mailboxes.

While I talk myself into getting the hell out of here, he notices my car parked a few feet below their driveway.

He taps on my window. "Who are you talking to?"

"Myself."

"About?" His finger motions downward.

I lower the window. "Calling you to say this is a bad idea."

"Nonsense." He leans down and kisses my lips. "I didn't want to wait 'til after dinner to taste you again. It's been driving me crazy all afternoon thinking about it."

I look up at him and smile into his baby blues. "I can't go in there. I come from a working, middle-class family. You're obviously a caviar kid."

"Maeva, please don't look at me that way. Are my parents wealthy? Yes. Am I? No. My dad makes sure to tell me that every day I wake up in *his* house." He reaches for my hand on the steering wheel. "Don't judge me for what they have."

I hear his plea but still resist getting out of the car.

"One day, I will be rich. And I'll buy you the house of your dreams. Whatever you want. Will you come and have dinner with me? Please?"

I take a deep breath. "The minute I feel small, or judged, or—"

He cuts me off. "It won't happen. I won't let that happen. My folks are good people. Come inside and meet them. The faster we get this over with, the sooner we get to be alone." He opens my car door and leads me inside.

6

___

DO TO ME

MAEVA

Song: "Do To Me" by H.E.R.

David's strong hand caresses mine as we enter the front room. An oversized imported rug lies below a shiny, black piano beside a dim lamp pointed toward sheet music on the holder above the keys. A massive European painting extends across the wall, and the voices of his family travel from down the hall.

David kisses the back of my hand. "You're gorgeous. I mean, you look pretty," he corrects himself with a shaky voice.

How cute. He's just as nervous as I am.

I lower my head and blush from the compliment, lightly trembling from nervousness creeping in as the voices of his family grow louder. We enter a well-lit bar area.

"Mom. Dad. I'd like for you to meet Maeva. Maeva, these are my parents, Mr. & Mrs. Boyd."

"Nice to meet you both," I stutter. "You have a beautiful home."

"Don't be nervous, dear. David has been talking about you

since the sun came up this morning. I couldn't wait to put a face with the name. And a pretty face it is."

Mrs. Boyd whisks me away from the men before I thank her. I look back at David, flummoxed.

"Are Dad and I allowed to come?" he asks her.

She chuckles and fans him off as he and his father slowly pace behind us. "People have so many different diets and eating habits these days, so I had our cook prepare a little of everything. Vegan, vegetarian, pescatarian, keto. You name it."

"It all sounds delicious."

I observe statues, wall paintings, and a chandelier hanging from a high ceiling on the way to the veranda. With the push of a button, two window shades lift, inviting the moon resting on the lake to romanticize our evening.

David's brother and sister join us at the table just before dinner is served.

I stare at the brother. "Aren't you the..."

David finishes my sentence. "Drummer. Yeah. Maeva, meet my big brother, Moe, and my sister, Amy. Moe, I'm sure you remember—"

Moe interrupts David. "The smoke show... I mean, nice to see you again, Maeva."

I say in a low tone, "Nice meeting you both."

"I'm not sure my little brother got any sleep last night." Moe taps David's arm. "Did you, lucky bastard?"

"Language," Mrs. Boyd warns.

Moe and Amy chuckle, and I withdraw in my seat of embarrassment.

Mr. Boyd clears his throat. "Don't make our guest uncomfortable. And don't tease your brother."

"We're not teasing him, Dad," Amy sasses her father. "Nice to meet you, by the way. Don't mind us. We give David hell all the time."

"Language," Mrs. Boyd grits through her teeth.

I struggle to make eye contact with everyone at the table. My shoulders slouch, and I shiver, awaiting the inquisition.

"Excuse the rudeness of my children. You're the first girl David has ever brought to dinner," Mrs. Boyd reveals.

"Am I?" I smile at David then direct my conversation to his parents. "Thank you for having me."

"It's our pleasure. David has been so focused on writing music since he was a child that he never had time for anyone, I suppose. Certainly not a relationship. I mean, there were girls, I imagine, but none of them ever made it this far. Yet, here you are after one day." His mother stops talking abruptly when Mr. Boyd raises his brow at her.

My nails dig into my hands below the table as I overanalyze Mrs. Boyd's remark. It was hard to decipher if it was a compliment or criticism. Denial or approval.

David cuffs my hand under the table. Sweat forms in my palms. He clutches them then takes control of the situation.

"Can we talk about something else?" He glares at his mother. "I promised Maeva tonight would be fun."

"As long as it's not religion or politics. We don't do that at the table," Mrs. Boyd warns her family with a steely voice without making eye contact. "Do we?"

"No, ma'am."

Mr. Boyd leads the conversation from the head of the table, making sure to mention the numerous charities they donate to, such as efforts in rebuilding Haiti, March of Dimes, and St. Jude. Idle chit-chat continues about his construction company with little mention of his gentrification participation that Amy calls out. She keeps the attack on her father's character, sharing her views on sexist America and their acceptance of David and Moe skipping college to chase their dreams as musicians, when she wasn't afforded the same opportunity.

Mrs. Boyd asks me a question to shut Amy up. "What school do you attend, Maeva?"

"I'll be attending RIT this fall, majoring in furniture design."

"Furniture design? Hmm, I've never given thought if a man or a woman designed our furniture. When did you know you wanted to pursue a career in...?"

"Wood-working. I think I've always known. I took really good care of my doll's furniture when I was little. And I drew designs of furniture in art class for most of my assignments. Then, one day, I took a table my mother no longer wanted and carved a mini living room set for my dollhouse."

"Really?"

"I sanded and painted the pieces. I believe that was my defining moment."

"Well, I'm impressed," says Mr. Boyd.

David grabs my hand above the table. "Isn't she great?"

Dinner comes to an end, and Moe and Amy clear the table while David and I stroll on the boardwalk behind their house. The moon is visibly bright, floating above us in a clear, midnight-blue sky. The night temperatures on the water encircle us with a breeze while we sit cozy on a wooden swing.

David wraps his arm around me. "You having a good time?"

"It started off a tad rough, but things leveled out."

"My mom shocked me tonight, to be honest. But I gave you my word. I've got your back."

"I appreciate how you steered the conversation. Thank you."

"You know what I realized in there?"

"You mean during my interview?" I kid. "What's up?"

"I don't know how old you are?"

"Nineteen last month," I answer then counter with burning questions of my own. "And you are?"

"Twenty-one."

"And you live where?"

"Here, with my parents. In the space above the garage. Is that cool?"

"Who am I to judge? I still live with mine."

"Are you weirded out meeting my family so fast?"

I chortle. "I've been wondering *what the hell am I doing here* all night, but I'm glad I came."

"So am I." He moans the melody to "Nothing Compares 2 U" then sings the hook. "I would have been hurt if you'd said no."

I shake myself of the daze his voice quickly put me in. "Hurt? Should we talk about how fast this seems to be moving?"

A vacant look crosses David's face. He avoids my question with a kiss. A sweet, delicate peck evokes a swarm of warm kisses under broken rays of moonlight beneath the canopy hovering over the swing. Sharing the same air, breathing in as he breathes out usurps my control over my body.

The pulse between my thighs throbs through my panties. I need to be touched. I want to be touched. By him. And I submit to the urges aching in my center.

My hands ease under his shirt and trace the ridges of his abs I imagined to be perfectly sculpted and inverted. My fingertips confirm my assumption, making my imagination run wild, and wetness drip from the apex of my peak.

David whispers in my mouth, "I want you."

His tongue tours my chin, then his mouth sucks on my neck. The straps of my dress fall off my shoulders as he tastes my skin from my collarbone to the edge of my shoulder blade. The beats per minute of my heart thumping relentlessly scares me to stop my madness.

"It's too soon," I say, pulling back to cool off. "I mean I want to, but I've never moved this fast before. There's so much we don't know about each other."

"I'll tell you anything you wanna know. Ask away." His lips warm my upper body.

I pant with lustful images of David making sweet love to me.

"Why do you want me so bad?" I pause his lips touring my flesh. "And dinner with your family?"

He gazes into my eyes and twirls my curls around his finger. I inhale, staring back at him, then exhale from the intensity of his eyes holding me captive.

"I felt a connection with you the moment you walked into The Murf. I couldn't take my eyes off you." His hand brushes my chin. "Like right now. My attraction to you is... I can't put it into words. It was like this power surged through me, and in my head, you felt what I was feeling too." He caresses my cheek. "Did you?"

I nod. "Your voice pulled me to you. I've never experienced anything like that before."

David's lips find their way back to mine. Passion charges through my veins, and I lose all my values as desolate growing urges override my willpower to behave.

His hands investigate my bra, pushing it down to pinch my nipples. I remove his left hand and place it on my thigh. He reads my mind and inches up the hem of my dress until I'm exposed to the breeze blowing from the lake.

"Ah," I sigh as the top of my panties gently fold.

David follows the rising temperature from my wet heat directing him where to touch. I sigh and press my hand against his chest as moans hum from my throat. His touch destroys any inkling I possess to resist him. And with ease, my back stiffens, and my thighs spread open.

I throb at his fingers sliding my panties to the side. They rub and pluck my folds like the strings on his guitar while our eyes lock to watch each other's reaction. My mouth parts open, and I whine, going insane at the extreme passions he's withdrawing from me.

He kisses me to cover the sounds of pleasure I can't forbear. It intensifies my arousal, and my legs begin to numb.

David sucks on my nipple then rests his cheek against mine. "Maeva, I don't want to stop."

I don't want him to. I want to feel him inside of me. Go all the way with him. Connect our forbidden parts the way his voice connects with my soul. Explore his manliness and bring the dreams I had hours ago to fruition. But not on the dock.

"Neither do I, but we can't do this here."

"I know." David composes himself. "Let's go to my room."

"So your parents can think less of me?"

"Technically, my room isn't a part of the main house."

Amy's voice appears behind us. "David!"

I lift the straps on my dress and lower the hem back to my feet. David stands to address her then sits back down when the bulge in his chinos hugs the zipper lining. I bite my bottom lip, lusting at his swollen knot.

"What's up, sis?"

"Mom wants you two to come inside. She's ready to serve her million desserts."

"We'll be right in." He mauls me with a hard kiss. "To be continued."

I wipe my mauve lipstick from his mouth. "I think I've gotten rid of the evidence."

He feels me up when I stand. "Let's go play nice for a little longer."

7

INSIDE FRIEND

DAVID

Song: "Inside Friend" by Leon Bridges

The back of her dress flows with the wind. My fingers cling to her waistline as a guide while my nose inhales the lavender and vanilla notes of her perfume enveloping around me. The part of me that craves her wants to tell Amy to get lost or send a message back up to the house that I was about to have the dessert I wanted.

As we walk back up to the house, my mind is filled with lovely, dirty images of us, making it hard to suppress the hard-on she's given me.

Ugh. Damn Mom and her desserts.

We join my family, already gathered in the kitchen. Maeva and I sit at the bar, sneaking looks at one another while Mom places a piece of chocolate pound cake in front of us.

"This time it came out real moist," she brags.

Amy, Moe, and I snicker.

"Mom, please don't say that ever again." Amy guffaws.

My hands hide my face as thoughts of the moisture between

Maeva's thighs arouse me, and a whiff of her essence on my fingers intoxicate the gentleman I was raised to be. I press them near my lips and inhale the sweet scent of drip until my mother burdens me to taste her cake.

I look at Maeva and wipe the icing from the top of my slice with that same finger. When I place it in my mouth, she squirms. Her shameful eyes beg me to stop teasing her, but the lust in my bones refuses to be tamed. I repeat my seductive gesture until she gives me a villainous grin, then I honor her nonverbal request and behave for the rest of the evening.

We entertain my family's shenanigans far longer than either of us want to. Eager to pick up where we left off, I announce Maeva and I are going for a drive.

I lift her inside my truck to cop a feel of her waistline. The look she gives me says she knows what I'm doing, so I hurry up to my side and drive us away from the home cameras and nosey neighbors looking out of the window when the motor in my truck fires up.

She rubs the back of my neck while I chauffeur her around the area. Both the engine of my truck and in my pants rev from her soft hands brushing against my skin. Her touch weakens and strengthens me simultaneously.

Neither of us speak, and I consider pulling off the main road to taste her sweet nectar in secluded woods and let my tongue do all the talking.

"David." Maeva pauses. "I'm not experienced."

I stop at the red light and turn to her. Her eyes look like they belong on a puppy in the light. Her breasts stand out for attention. I crave to give them the warm caress they deserve but respectfully keep my hands to myself.

"Are you saying you're a—a..."

"A virgin? No. I left a boyfriend behind in South Carolina. I mean, we're not together or anything. It's just...we only did it a few times, and he's the only person I've ever been with." Her voice lowers. "I can't promise you I know what I'm doing or if I will please you the way I'm sure you're used to."

"The way *I'm* used to?"

She bites her nails. "Forget I said anything."

I kiss her fingertips then gnaw on them until she giggles. "You wanna tell me what you mean by that?"

Maeva drags her hands down to my zipper. "I don't want your parents to hate me or judge me. But I'm ready to see your room."

The light turns green, and I speed through it. The coast is clear of the local authorities, so I make an illegal U-turn quickly and park my truck a few feet away from the view of the security cameras at the house.

"Maeva, my parents wouldn't have a problem with you in my room, but I don't want you to worry. So, we're going to sneak inside. They'll never know we made it back. Okay?"

She nods, and I steal another kiss from her.

"Let's go."

Quietly, we tiptoe to the side of the house. Maeva giggles uncontrollably, forcing us to lean our bodies flat against the house until she settles down.

We proceed to enter. I unlock the side door and slip us both inside the garage then slink open the door to the house. Maeva covers her mouth to muffle her snickers. Dad's voice carries from the kitchen, and Mom's laughter cackles faintly from the pantry.

"Coast is clear," I whisper.

Quickly, we close the door behind us. I glide up the stairs with Maeva in front of me and grab the sides of her waist to stop at the second step from the top.

"That one creaks," I tell her.

Maeva lifts her dress above her ankles and overextends her stunning, golden-brown legs to the top of the stairs. I stare at them, envisioning how I'll spread them wide in the air.

She waits for me to follow her, teasing me with a dance at the top. I laugh below my breath and pull myself up with the rail then lead her into my space.

She locks the door behind us. The lights from my sound system give my room a dark-green hue.

I approach her. "I swear you're stunning in any light."

Her tongue draws mine into her mouth. She's a real-life wet dream gracing my room with lips that feel made specifically for me. Her curvy physique presses against the door, and I step forward as far as my hips will allow to grind my ready bone on her throbbing mound.

"I have never wanted anyone as badly as I want you right now."

She groans. "Promise you'll be gentle...at first."

My dick nearly bursts through the seams of my trousers. I press it firmly against her, hunching her into the wood of the door. She pants and moans in between our kisses, rocking her ready pussy forward for more pressure.

My hands work her dress up to her thighs, and I wedge two fingers inside her heat.

"David," she calls out, dripping on my knuckles.

I slide her straps down, drop to my knees, pull her dress to the floor, and lick her sweet nectar, smacking my lips and nibbling on her tender flesh.

"I knew you'd taste like sugar," I say, staring at her pussy in the low light.

Maeva's body tightens in my hands. I tug on her thighs and slick her entrance with my tongue, then I look up at her to see her face. Her chest concaves from holding her breath, and her fingers are wrapped around the front of her neck. Passionate hums escape her slightly parted lips. Her face looks like it did on the dock. Tense. Pleased. Eager. And exotic.

My hands slide to her ass. I hold her steady with her warm embrace deep in my mouth, juicing her fountain with her mounted above me like the flat screen on my wall.

Slowly, I press the bottom of my mouth below her hood, and slither my tongue hard, fast, up and down her clit. She comes relentlessly in my oral bowl, jolting in my taut grip.

I raise her body higher in the air. She clings to the wall behind her as I lick and slick her mound in rotation.

"I want you now," she begs.

I continue to water her, thrilled by her moans turning into grunts from impatience, then lower her to her feet. I rise and witness her perfect silhouette in the low light. She glistens in the dark, like fairy dust and newfound gold.

My shirt flies above my head, and she steps forward, running her hands down my chest to below my abs. Her fingers unbutton my pants and unravel my zipper past the bulge of my cock. The zip trail splits open, freeing my manhood. It springs forward and pokes her abdomen with a tinge of my spoils at the tip.

I swell barbarously from the touch of her skin brushing against my head. She jerks when my fluid seeps on her.

"It's okay." I reach for her face and pacify her lips with a kiss. "Gentle at first. I promise."

She bats her eyes and studies my drill, stroking my base with soft tugs. I'm in her hands and at her mercy, buckling at the knees.

"Protection," she mutters.

I coach her to the bed and lay her on her back, reach in my drawer and tear the plastic with my teeth. The condom slaps at the end of my shaft, and I position my dick on her sugar walls, rolling it in a circle until my head parts her flesh.

She shivers beneath me.

I pause to rub my cheek with hers then sigh with controlled patience. "Hold onto me," I tell her.

She rests her hands on my shoulders, and I plow my way inside her snug, soaking wet center. Her moisture nearly soaks through the latex, and I regret I didn't beg to slide in it raw.

Her face, her body, her personality, and now her tight pussy have me thinking careless thoughts of shredding the bag and feeling her pure flesh, getting her pregnant, and making her mine for eternity.

She's too good for that. Don't do it, I convince myself, memorizing the way she looks taking all of me when I squeeze my full cock inside.

My strokes begin gentle, the way I promised, but when I hear her first grunt of pleasurable pain from my dick, I let loose on her pussy and give her the pounding I dreamed of.

I pick up the pace and expand my territory. She gyrates below me, thrusting her hips forward to welcome every inch of my wood inside her world, edging me on to hit every corner and every cut of her saturated glory.

Lowering my chest on top of hers, I apply pressure to the top of her canal, knocking and scraping the sides of her boat with the tip of my head.

She whispers, "Oh God," and my ego multiplies.

"Is this what you wanted?" I ask, going deeper into her gulf stream.

She squeezes my pecs. "Yes."

"I claim your pussy? Say it's mine," I demand, winding my wood like a tornado.

Maeva shrieks and digs her nails into my arms. "It's mine." She grins at me devilishly.

I graze her bottom lip with my teeth and wipe away her smirk. "I couldn't hear you." I unleash more powerful strokes until she says what I want to hear. "Tell me you're mine."

"I'm yours."

"Damn right you are."

I poke her with steadfast jabs, stirring her golden pot with my dick like a spoon. She whines in my ear and calls my name, the good Lord, and mutters a few *fucks* in between.

Within a day, she's inspired two songs in my journal—a number sure to rise by the end of the night.

She bites my shoulder then moans in a tone deeper than her real voice. I lift her ass off the bed and hold her love closer than close to my zone, pressing us firmly together as I damn near choke exerting myself.

I can imagine what it feels like to touch those walls bare. Countdown until she lets me.

8

WITH YOU

MAEVA

Song: "With You" by Monica

*A*live. Ashamed. Afraid. Amazed.

David's inexplicable hold on me fills me with fright. I lie next to him and feel unrecognizable. Wild. Risky.

Thoughts of straddling him like a horse, breaking the bed, and fucking him like a porn star keep me entertained while I listen to him catch his breath. I'm trapped in a tight lock, impossible to escape his arms.

My mind wonders if I would have caved and let him fuck me on the boardwalk. Would Amy have caught us? Was I so far gone that I would have let him have his way with me while his family watched from the main house? The taboo of it all and the smell of his sex sweat makes me want him again.

His hands and his mouth feel like summer on my skin, and my cup runneth over with urges to drip on him like I did when the breeze breathed on my nipple as he sucked it.

I feel insatiable in his bed and want more moments like our perilous stint on the bench out back—and soon.

David molds my body and takes my mind to places I didn't

know existed. Places where pain is pleasurable. And lust feels like love. His voracious virility has been injected in my veins like a hit of smack. I see colors and envision I'm running naked in a field of perfect penises, mimicking the motion of his lumber circling inside me. They're all tawny, full, and engorged like a mushroom at the tip, sprouted in a meadow in the countryside just for me.

What the fuck does this man have me thinking? I laugh to myself.

"Baby," he whispers, breathing heavily with one hand resting on his chest and the other placed on my thigh.

Damn, I'm baby already?

"Yeah?" I answer.

"I don't know what possessed you to come to the bar last night, but I now understand what people mean when they say the stars were aligned. Either that, or I'm just one lucky beau."

I titter. "And to think I almost stayed home and did my laundry."

He turns to face me, leans down, and we kiss. "I don't want to imagine not seeing you walk through that door."

His fingers massage my scalp and run through my hair. I don't know which is better—him sucking my rose like a plate of ribs, stroking me into another dimension, or relaxing me with a sensual kneading that makes my back wilt and body go limp.

My phone chirps, lost somewhere on the floor.

"I should answer that," I say, not moving a muscle.

His shiatsu spell has me immobilized. I'm a prisoner to his hands and can't take my eyes off the hairs waving in patterns on his chest or stop listening to the pounding of his heart slowing down to normal.

The scent of his chest magnetizes my arousal, and I want to jump on him, but the sensation of the rubdown prevents me from acting on impulse while the beeping sound ruins my motivation.

"She's going to call until I answer." I manage to wiggle a hand free.

"Tell her you're not coming home tonight."

He loosens his hold, and I spring to the floor, searching through our clothes for my phone. David teases me with a song as I comb through our apparel.

"Maev's not coming home tonight."

I toss his shirt at his face. "Quiet before your parents hear you."

I dial my mother with my eyes glued on him rolling the condom from his penis and wiping himself with the shirt.

He throws it in the garbage, mimicking a basketball shot. "Two points," he whispers and jumps up from the bed.

Ma answers. "Did they have to catch, kill, and cook the food?"

"No, ma'am. But we did have several courses."

She scoffs.

"I'm calling to let you know I'm on my way," I mutter with David kissing my back and rubbing his cock on my ass cheeks.

Ma's voice deepens with disapproval. "So, it went well, then?"

"Yes, ma'am," I answer her, swatting David away.

She grunts. "Well, drive safe. I'll expect you shortly."

I hang up the phone and push David back on the bed. A cowboy hat rests on the back of the headboard. I set it on my head then spread my thighs across his. His nature bounces side to side.

"Maeva, you're starting something lying on me like this."

"I can tell. I'm using you as a towel since you didn't give me one."

He grins. "Use me all you want. And remind me to put that hat on you next time we... Better yet, I say we go ahead and make next time right now."

I tap his leg.

He groans and slides his hands down my waistline. "Middle drawer."

I hop off him and help myself. "How are you going to get me out of here?"

"Didn't you hear my song? You're spending the night."

"Whatever." I slap the elastic of my panties in place.

"What I'd give to have a picture of you just like that."

"Where's your phone?"

He sprawls to the floor and pulls it out of his jeans. I tilt the hat low enough the cover my eyes and pose with my back facing him so my breasts aren't in the shot.

"I'll be staring at this all night."

"Just promise me that won't get out."

"For my eyes only."

"Now, how about you work on the plan to get me to my car without giving your parents the impression I'm a cheap slut. I need to hit the road so my Ma won't worry."

He reaches for me with his manhood, ready for a second row. "My people won't say anything if you stay over, but I understand your mom wanting you to come home." He slips on a clean shirt while I pull up my dress.

"I don't think I can ever spend the night here. Me, doing the walk of shame in front of your parents—not gonna happen." I step into my sandals. "Maybe in a hotel."

"If that's what it takes." He squeezes me tight. "I'll figure something out."

I place his hat on the door handle, and we head out. David lifts me over the noisy step then pins me on the wall of the stairwell.

"I hate that you're leaving me," he whispers, kissing me passionately on my lips.

I whisper back, "If this were your place, I'd stay all night and face the consequences."

The grip of his hand around my waist softens. "I miss you already," he says then escorts me outside where we run into Moe standing near the garage door.

Moe inhales a long toke of weed and narrows his eyes at me. A heavy cloud of smoke blows from his lips, then he smirks.

"Good God, you've got it bad," he says to David.

David punches his shoulder. "Shut up."

I bury my face in my hands while the two of them shove each other.

Moe smiles at me. "No need and sneak off, lil' lady. Mom's waiting on you inside to take food home to your folks."

"Really? I was afraid she knew we were upstairs."

"Nah. She thinks you two are still out on a drive." He inhales another toke. "I'm the only one who knows you two were up there." He pats David on the back.

They share a brotherly look, then David takes me back inside the house through the front door.

"Mom!" David shouts. "Maeva wants to tell you good night!"

We snicker like toddlers, leaning into each other in the open foyer. Mr. and Mrs. Boyd appear around the corner from the bar area of the house.

"You two have a good time?" Mrs. Boyd inquires.

"Yes, ma'am," I answer. "Thank you for inviting me into your lovely home."

"It was our pleasure, Maeva. I wrapped up some leftovers for you. I'll go grab them."

Mr. Boyd approaches and offers his hand.

"It was nice to finally meet one of David's friends." His grip is firm. "If this knucklehead gives you any problems, you come and tell his old man. I'll get on him for ya."

"She's not just a friend, Dad." David takes my hand from his father's grasp. "It's cool to call you my girlfriend, right?"

I blush at the word and study the glow in his blue eyes. "Yes." I chuckle.

"Well, then, I guess we'll be seeing more of you 'round these parts, Miss Maeva."

David lowers his head to mine as Mrs. Boyd returns with a zippered nylon bag full of food. My eyes widen, wondering if she thinks my family is a charity case or if she's naturally generous.

"Take this, dear. I hate for food to go to waste."

"Thank you. I'll be sure to get this bag back to you."

"Oh, don't worry about it, dear. I have a pantry full of them." She hugs me goodbye.

David opens my car door and leans in to kiss me, holding onto my lips, hesitant to close the door.

"I feel like I should follow you home. I regret letting you leave the bonfire so late and not seeing you made it home safe."

"I'm sure I'll be fine, but if it makes you feel better, sure. Why not?"

His face lights up brighter than the stars shining above us. He jogs down to his truck parked a few feet away and talks to me on the phone all the way to my side of town.

He walks me to the door, and we share a lovely, silent moment staring into each other's eyes on the steps.

"I'd invite you in, but I'm almost positive my mother is asleep on the couch in her pajamas..."

He reels me in close, compelling me with forehead kisses.

I attempt to cool him down. "Would your mother be offended if I sent her bag home with you? I'm not sure what to do with it."

David rests his forehead against mine. "Maeva, I'm not thinking about my mom or that bag right now. When will I see you again?"

"I guess whenever you're free, and when I'm not looking after my Dad."

"On the drive over here, I got to thinkin'. The band and I are playing in the city on Friday night. What if you came along? You can check out the show, and we can make a weekend of it."

The seriousness in his eyes sweeping over me and the desperation in his voice jumpstarts me to say, "I like that idea."

"So, it's a yes?"

"Yes."

I TAKE SLICES OF CAKE, leftover pie, carrot salad, and mounds of fruit from Mrs. Boyd's bag and force them to fit inside the fridge. Ma is asleep on the sofa, as I expected.

I tap her on the shoulder, help her to her feet when she wakes, then walk with her to her bedroom.

Pop is propped up on the bed when we enter. "Sounded like the boy has a nice set of wheels."

"He's a country boy with a country truck. And what are you doing awake? You know you both don't have to wait up for me. I'm not in high school anymore. I'll be twenty on my next birthday."

Ma rolls next to my dad, and they both chuckle.

Pop points to me. "Marva, do you see it now?"

"Oh, I see it alright." She cuddles in my father's arms.

"See what?" I demand.

"Trouble," my mother answers. "Sounds like—which one are you seeing?—Bo or Luke, saw to it that you got home safe. I guess he's alright people."

My face wrinkles. "Who are Bo and Luke?"

My parents burst into laughter at my ignorance of the names. Pop fans himself to calm down then taps my mother on her hand.

"Marva, behave."

Ma guffaws until she turns red then continues to query me. "How was his family?"

"Everyone was nice. I had a good time."

"And?"

"And David invited me to his show this weekend. I told him I would go. It requires travel," I lie.

My parents look at each other.

"By yourself?" Ma furrows her brows.

"Ma, no disrespect, but I'm going. I was being respectful by telling you in advance."

Her eyes slight me as she attempts to rise up from my father's embrace. He tightens his grip and holds her back.

"I'm sure it'll be fun." His brows curve. "But we'd like to meet the boy first."

"I'm sure I can make that happen. Good night."

Upon my exit, I turn off the light and listen to their subdued giggles from behind the closed door. I regret lying to them about the trip, since Nashville is a hop and a skip away, but nothing is gonna stop me from seeing the man I let defile me in my weakest hour and would soon have to leave behind.

9

COME AWAY WITH ME

DAVID

Song: "Come Away With Me" by Norah Jones

*B*etween rehearsals for the show and Maeva taking care of her father 'round the clock, our relationship has been on our phones all week. We text more than practice how to make a love child, so when the sun rises on Friday, I wake up happier than a kid with cake when I should be focusing on the show.

I worm through the morning traffic to claim our hotel reservation downtown, hightail it back to Souse's garage to help pack up the van, then swing by Maeva's to meet her folks.

I find it hard to maintain my composure after missing her for five torturous days and five lonesome nights since she let me jump her bones. I stand in her living room, antsy like a fiend too broke to get his fix, fumbling my words from the way Mrs. Martin is staring me down.

Mr. Martin is all smiles and cool about me pursuing Maeva, but Mrs. Martin...her eyes have been cutting me like a samurai sword since the moment Maeva invited me in.

Her questions put me on the spot. My pits were already

sweaty, but she's about to make them drip, quizzing me as if I'm on a job panel interview. Thankfully, Maeva butts in.

"Ma." She hands me her overnight bag. "I've given you his last name, his parents' address, and you've met him, so you know what he looks like. We need to hit the road so he can make it in time for his rehearsal. I'll be fine."

"I give you my word. I'll look after Maeva."

"From the stage?" Mrs. Martin corners me.

"Maaaaa."

"We have security, ma'am. I won't let anything happen to her."

"I'm in good hands. Love you both." Maeva gets me out of hell's kitchen.

I throw her bag in the back of my truck and start off the weekend with a long kiss at the stop sign at the end of her road.

"I damn near did that in front of your folks. I missed you, baby."

A car pulls up behind us and blows their horn.

"Go around!" I shout.

They swerve around us and give us the finger.

Maeva pulls back and wipes her lips. "We better go." The print in my jeans causes her lips to part. "And I missed you too."

It's taking everything in me not to swing by the hotel first as she teases me with a knee stroke. I turn the AC on high to keep us cool, and we meet the guys at the venue.

While we unload the equipment and set up the stage, Maeva makes herself scarce, taking pictures and touring the space. Every now and then, I catch a glimpse of her walking around and making friends with security and the staff. I do a good job focusing on the task at hand with the band, even though she's a distraction. But as the clock winds down and we complete our run through, I get a second wind, as if all the running around and the travel I've done isn't taxing.

Time quickly winds down, and we head to the hotel for a quick change. I show her our pad for the weekend. The glimmer in her eyes says she approves. She spins around the room as I place our bags on the table below the mirror in the den.

"This is us until Sunday." My eyes are glued to her wiping off the remote with a Clorox wipe. "What are you doing?"

"Probably freaking you out. I have a slight touch of OCD. Can't be in filth. And if you saw the program I saw on how hotels look clean but are—sorry. I wish I had never seen that show." She draws the curtains together as I close in on her. "You did good. The room is lovely. I was praying you didn't put us in a motel and I'd have to pretend I was cool with it." She chuckles until my hands squeeze her toned waist.

"I wouldn't do you like that."

"That's good to know. You might not like me anymore once you hear me bitch and moan."

"I can help you with the moan part." I kiss her neck and palm the seat of her jeans.

"Ooh," she purrs. "Sounds good to me."

I plant a wet kiss on her lips. "But you deserve more than a quickie. And I plan to spend time tending to you."

"As long as you deliver."

"I promise." I gently bite her lip. "I gave the band my word that I would be present before and after the show."

"You sure I won't be a distraction tonight? I don't mind hanging back and waiting for you here."

My johnson tests my strength. I place her hands on it and observe her alluring eyes.

"I want you there, but if you choose to stay in, this is what you can expect when I get back."

She rolls her fingers around my swelling knot and cuffs it in her hand. "You're lucky I'm a patient girl." She grazes my bottom lip with her teeth. "I know you need those babies for the show tonight. I wouldn't dare damage them."

A sinful sneer curves on my lips as my phone vibrates in my

pocket. "I need them for two shows." I pick her up and throw her on the bed.

She signals for me to come to her, biting on her bottom lip and slowly running her fingers up and down her thighs. "Have a good show tonight."

I crawl on top of her and kiss her hard. "You're sending me on stage with a loaded clip. You're gonna pay for that when I get back."

"I can't wait for your second performance. Go do your thing."

THE BAND APPLAUDS me when I walk through the turnstile doors, joshing me for not answering the call.

"Ten minutes to come down. I called it," Souse admits.

"I'd say that time is about right," Moe jokes.

I laugh. "Maybe for you."

Moe drives us over to Brown's down in Germantown, where a few of the locals and supporters from the Murf welcome us whenever we come to the city. I throw one beer back while the gang mingles with the usuals, then I round up the boys to leave for the show.

The hall is jam-packed to capacity. A fight breaks out near the end of the first song in our set. Security removes the rebels, and the partygoers shout for us to pick up where we left off by singing the tune in unison.

We feed off of their energy then set them ablaze with our cover of Brooks & Dunn's "Play Something Country" to get the party restarted. From there, we can't and *don't* do anything wrong, pulling out our big guns one after the other. Five songs later, we bring it home to a roaring crowd, thankfully filled with the locals singing along to our first local hit.

Keeping my promise, I hang back with the fellas and mingle

with the fans, take pictures for the press, and fraternize with the other bands shooting the shit once the crowds disperse.

While packing up the equipment, Souse suggests we keep the party going down on Whiskey Row.

"You boys go do what you wanna. I'm headed to the hotel."

Souse hounds me. "This girl's really got you going."

"What's it to you? I'm handling my business, writing new songs, and pulling my weight. The show was phenomenal, and now it's over. Why are you creating a problem?"

Moe steps between Souse and me. "Calm down, bro. We've got three weeks until the audition for the label. Don't fuck up your voice over this one's jealousy."

"Jealous! Why do you think I'm jealous?"

"We were all looking at that broad when she walked through the door. We all knew she was in a place where she didn't belong, and we all wanted a piece. But she chose this numbnuts," Lim jokes to lighten the mood. "They always go for the front man."

"*That broad*' is my lady," I say with my chest.

"Call it luck of the singer," Souse adds.

"Speak for yourself. I do pretty well with the birds," Moe brags. "Matter of fact, I'll pass on the after-party. I've got plenty to choose as is." He points to the women hanging out in packs near the van. "If we're done with this, I'll be on my way. But who's taking the van?"

Lim shoves Moe. "I'm coming with you, and I say *we* take the van."

I chime in. "Did you guys forget our equipment is in there?"

Everyone grows silent.

"I say we ride with them." Lim points to the group of girls. "You in, Souse?"

"I'm not a charity case. I have a sure shot lined up for later. But yeah, I say we ride with those chicks, and David can park the van at the hotel. You fools wouldn't know what to do with them anyhow." Souse nudges me. "We good?"

"I'm not the one with issues."

"All I'm saying is we're on the verge of our big break. This ain't the time for a relationship. We've got to be social with the ladies. Our lead can't be standoffish like you were tonight," Souse points out.

I hop in the truck. "Have fun tonight, ladies." I throw leftover beer cans and half eaten candy bars at the guys.

"If we don't make it back to the hotel tonight, we'll send the drop where to pick us up in the morning."

"Fat chance!" I yell out the window.

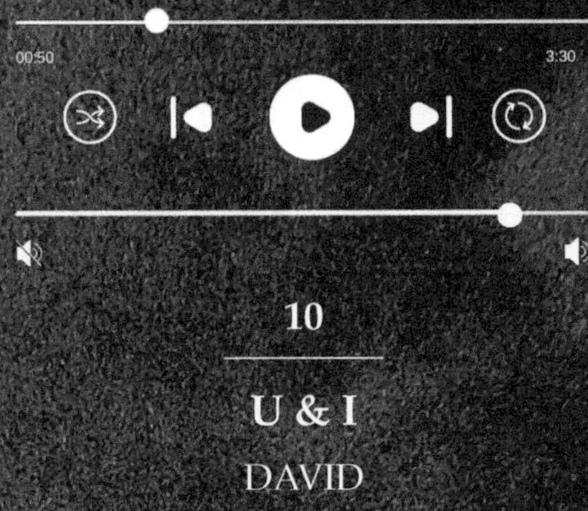

10

U & I

DAVID

Song: "u & I" by Jodeci

My breath is taken away at Maeva lying on the bed, ready to give it a go. Naked and oiled like a Greek goddess, she's posed with a book in her hand, smiling at me on the side of her mouth.

"How'd it go, Cowboy?"

"Uh, a fight broke out, but we rocked it." I lay my case against the wall and take off my shirt. "I see it's going well in here." I lean down to kiss her. "I'm covered in dried up sweat and smoke, baby. Let me get this stench off me so I can take care of my second performance tonight."

Maeva lifts from the bed and unzips my blue jeans before I can pull away. She's got a twirl in her eyes, screaming she wants me right now. I stare into her eyes as my hands slide with ease down her shiny, slick torso and palm her throbbing soft and wet with a stronghold.

The front of my wrist rubs, deep and rigorous, against her clit. She closes her eyes, on the verge of liberation, and falls on the bed.

I hover above her, and my knees shiver, succumbing to her low screams of passion.

She reaches for the headboard in ecstasy. "I'm close," she sighs.

"I love the way you look when you come. Come for me, baby." My wrist relaxes and gently massages her sweet spot.

Maeva firmly presses on my shoulders, groaning, squirming, and thrusting upward. I lock my wrist and apply pressure with the bone. She whines my name, and I hold my position steady, sealing her wet folds with pleasured torture.

I intensify rubbing her clit relentlessly as my fingers slip inside and scissor her hole. Her spearmint breath pants in delight, and she presses on my hand.

"Hold it there! Don't move it! Don't move it!" she orders, closing her eyes.

I obey her command and nibble on her breast, sending her into a jolting revolution. "You like that?"

She nods, holding her breath.

"What about this?" I reverse the direction my fingers strum inside of her.

The pounding of her heart grows louder. Her eyes open and meet mine. She exhales and breaks the silence with gratifying groans. Her body quakes, and I smile at the look of paradise on her face.

I roll my fingers around her drip, and temptation conquers me. I slide between her goldmine, trembling from her touch, quickly learning if there is a heaven, she has it between her legs.

Maeva gasps at my insertion, pushing upward on my chest. I grumble a sinful groan with every stroke, turning her brown skin and my white flesh into a colorful canvas. The most beautiful, vivid image before my eyes.

She owns me.

I lift her legs above my shoulders and dive deeper into her

ocean. The fragility of her shivering legs resting against my chest brings out the hidden animal in me.

I growl when her body locks tight against the sheets, and her thighs firmly choke my neck as I swim in her sea of love.

The wilder I stroke, the more vocal and wetter she becomes. I see my future in her eyes as she rains all over my cock, and I holler when my rifle shoots bullets inside of her, staking my claim in her land of waterworks, giving myself to her completely in this moment. I dare anyone to try and come between us.

11

___

ELUSIVE

MAEVA

The connection between us deepens with an unbreakable gaze and David's hitched breath against my shoulder. The sound of his beating heart keeps me alert. The smell of his cologne, sweat, and dried smoke leads me to run us a bath.

As he rests on the bed, I fill the tub half full then dip my toes inside the warmth of the water. David slips in behind me and sits me between his legs, massaging my shoulders while I lie back on his chest.

I lift the knob with my foot and stop the water from pouring in when it reaches just below my breasts. The sensation of the steam tending to my pleasured passage pulsating from the pillage and the caress of David's hands kneading my arms and shoulders forces me to sink deeper and melt away in bliss.

This moment feels surreal. Better than the many ways I imagined it all week. The two of us alone, about to spend our first night together without any rules, judgment, or interruption.

"I could get used to this," he says.

"It does feel nice."

He kisses the side of my face, humming a tune I'm unfamiliar with.

"I don't know that one."

"It's something new I'm working on."

The rhythm dances against my skin as he returns to the tune while kissing my neck. I reach back and run my wet fingers in his hair, and the melody fades.

In the soap lathered across my breast, David scrolls a D & M in the foam. "Dave & Maev."

"Is that the name of the song?"

"I haven't given it a name yet, but that'd be a good one." He drones a new beat. "Maeva, how far away is your school?"

"Far." I pause. "Like half a day to drive. Why?"

"Thinking ahead and wishing I could keep you all to myself." He nibbles on my loose hair strands laid against his face.

"Someone sounds selfish." I chuckle. "What are we doing tomorrow?"

"I'm taking you out and about town. We're going to eat, shop, and hopefully come back to the room and repeat what we just did if I have my way. That is, if I can stand tomorrow after making love to you all night."

"Don't make promises you can't keep," I joke.

An hour later, I eat the very words I spoke. On the cusp of a relaxing, well-deserved sleep, David's third leg stands at attention from a sudden movement of my inner thighs twitching. It pokes my lower back, tapping above my line like the foot pedal of a bass drum.

"Maev..."

"Hmm?"

He continues to wake me with soft kisses to my neck. "I wanna see how you fuck."

His request turns me on. I mount him like Prairie Rose of the west, rolling my hips to my very own satisfaction, watching him gasp as he motions my waist back and forth.

"That's how you like it?" I ask, grinding him slow to prolong his eruption.

He grins then sighs. "I told you I could get used to this."

"I'm starting to believe you."

"If only you could see how fucking gorgeous you look above me. I want to wake up like this every morning."

I quickly slip him out and turn around. He pushes upward back inside of me, and I ride him harder, squatted with my feet glued next to his hips in reverse cowgirl. His hands guide my ass around and side to side until the pounding drains the last of my energy. David recognizes he has weakened me and lifts my fatigued body by the waist.

"Ah," I moan from the sensitivity of my pussy placed on his mouth.

Soft licks soothe the pain, weaving a pearl tongue from my entrance. I shiver above him, held firm in his strong hands, caught in a rapture of ecstasy so good I don't want him to stop.

"Fuck!" I whimper. "Finish me off."

David lifts me to my knees and explores my epicenter deeper with a rippling tongue. "Gentle," he says, watering my garden with precision. "At first." He jabs deep and hard, thoroughly plowing my hidden lips with fast circular strokes, long dicking me from the back until I pass out.

Morning passes, and our plans derail. The morning sunrise has been missed and breakfast long gone. We leave our love nest in late afternoon, hungry from the bedroom festivities, and settle for lunch at the hotel.

We salvage the little time left to hit the streets after I make a quick drugstore run before he shows me the city.

David's face lights up as he schools me during the tour of the Country Music Hall of Fame and Museum.

I pinch his hand. "You'll be in here one day."

His posture wilts, and his eyes get lost staring at a gold record on the wall, resembling a child in front of a class on career day, discussing what they're gonna be when they grow up. I stand next to him and wait for his daze to be broken.

"Sorry 'bout that." He reaches for my hand. "You ready to move on?"

"Whenever you are."

My history lesson continues with a stroll down Broadway, a drive by of the famous Blue Bird Café minutes away from Music Row, then a brief visit to the Opry attractions and shopping mall on the other side of town.

"I wasn't thinking straight," he says. "I should have taken you to try the town staple."

"Which is?"

"Nashville Hot Chicken."

"Honestly, I'm exhausted and still full from lunch. Say you'll whisk me away and bring me back another time to try it."

"I give you my word I will." He kisses me. "Sleep's calling me. Somebody kept me up past my bedtime." He squeezes my ass. "Room service and a movie?"

"Sounds perfect to me."

"Hop on."

I climb on his back and hug his shoulders throughout my carriage ride to the car. We skimp on our room service order, and fall asleep during the movie, waking in the middle of the night to a quiet, dimly lit room.

Our eyes meet briefly, initiating the proper way to bridge the night with Sunday morning. Hours later, I wake up to sticky sheets and David's arms draped around me.

"Back to reality," he says, smiling at me.

I roll on top of him. "I enjoyed this. I enjoyed you."

He kisses my nose. "I won't be satisfied until this becomes the norm for us."

The sentiment of his words sounds nice. I stare into his eyes, reliving the moment of his explosive performance, but also dreading the month of August quickly approaching and wishing time would slow down.

12

I'LL CALL YOU BACK

MAEVA

"That sure was a lot of kissing for the neighbors to see," Ma fusses.

My lips can't resist turning up as I walk past her. She scoffs and rolls her eyes on her way out of the living room, leaving me alone with Pop sitting on the sofa.

"Did you have a good time?" he asks, shaking his head at my mother.

"It was fun. Very different from what I was expecting." I cover my lie with another lie. "David promises to take me back when he's not performing so I can see more than a show."

"Glad to hear you enjoyed yourself. Even happier you're home safe to grace your old man with that sunshine smile of yours. How did David's band perform?"

"Amazing. You should come see them with me sometime. I'd invite Ma too, but she'd cramp our style," I whisper.

Pop giggles. "I'll take your word for it and leave the partying to you young folk. I'm sure he's as good as you say he is, but I bet he's no Smokey."

"I'm going to tell him you said that." I kiss my father on the cheek. "Smokey."

Ma pretends she isn't eavesdropping when I make it to my bedroom. I stand still in the doorway and wait for her to call my name.

Right on cue, she hollers, "Maeva!"

I drop my head and prepare myself not to react to her rehearsed lecture.

Casually, I stroll into her room. She sits on her side of the bed with worried eyes, raised brows, and back-to-back sighs blowing from her mouth.

At the foot of her bed, I shake my head at the look on her face. Her cheeks flinch from a combination of a smile and a smirk, and her arms are crossed tighter than a rope.

I purposely don't blink, hoping she'll crack, but she's unyielding, staring back at me until I'm the first to fold.

"Why don't you like him?" I ask her.

"What did I tell you about asking questions to answers you already know?"

"I have no idea what you have against him," I voice lightly. "You met him one time, and I haven't seen any red flags, Ma."

"I looked up the address you gave me. What are you doing getting mixed up with people like him? He's from a completely different world. A class of people that look down on people like us."

"Ma, I thought the same thing, but his family was nothing but nice to me."

"Humph. Trust me, dumpling, his people would stop at nothing to break you two up if this fling were to get serious. I say this to protect you and because I love you. Not to hurt you. No mother likes seeing their child hurt."

"I hear you. But you're wrong."

"I wish I were, Maeva Martin."

Oh God. The full name.

My mother's lack of trust in my relationship with David hurts, but it doesn't deter my feelings. I realize, while listening to her, that I have fallen in love with a country boy, told him I was his, and her worry and assumptions couldn't stop me from loving him.

Riding high from an exciting weekend, I head back to my room with the image of her lips pressed tightly together tattooed on my brain. I close my door and dial up my best friends, Michelle and Nya, back home in Charleston.

"How did it go?" Michelle asks.

I whisper, "Add Nya on the line so I only have to say this once."

"Why are you talking so low?"

"You know why."

"Damn, your mother is still a smother?" Michelle laughs. "Hold on."

Nya answers her line. "What up?"

"Maev has something she wants to tell us."

"'*Sup* bitches!" Nya shrieks.

"I'm back from my special weekend."

"Girl, go to the car so you can stop whispering." Nya laughs.

As I open my door, I see my mother's shadow in the reflection of light in the hallway.

I knew she was listening.

I chuckle to myself, then shout, "I'm outside!"

"Don't feel bad. Your mama's not the only one trippin'. Mine reminded me my curfew still stands after I got home last night. Next summer, I'm definitely staying in the dorm," Michelle rants.

Nya clears her throat. "And this is why I said we should have all gone to the same college and *got* an apartment off campus. That's what I'm doin' when I go back to Maryland."

"So, how did it go?" Nya and Michelle both ask.

"Jinx. Buy me a Dr. Pepper," Michelle says first.

"I'll buy you both a Dr. Pepper if y'all would shut up and listen."

"Shit," they both say. "My bad."

"Neither one of you better say jinx right now. I have a serious question. How can I be sure this man ain't taking me for a ride?"

Nya cackles. "You can't."

"What street dreams did this boy promise?" Michelle asks. "And shit, send us the picture already. I'd like to know the face of the person I'm gonna talk shit about."

"He hasn't promised me anything. But being with him just feels different."

"How would you know, Maev? You've been with one guy."

"Two."

The collective gasps over the line sound like cicada frequencies.

Michelle's voice lowers. "You already fucked that man?"

I can't speak from smiling.

"Hello?" Nya chimes in.

"I did."

"Look at that, Chelle, the last one to get plucked is turnin' into a slut before our very eyes," Nya jokes. "How is he? Hung like a horse? Please say he's hung like a horse."

"None of your business."

"What? This guy has you holdin' secrets from *us*? Please don't say you're in love with him after one week."

Michelle adds on to the insult. "*Innit.*"

The phone goes silent as I refuse to answer Nya's abrasive line of questioning and bitchy attitude. I lay the phone on my lap as tears bubble in my eyes.

"Maeva! We're playin' witchu! Maeva!"

"What?"

"Oh shit." Nya's voice loses its jokey edge. "You *do* love him."

Michelle breathes into the phone. "But you didn't tell him that. Right?"

"No, I didn't tell him that, but I'm pretty sure he feels the same way."

Michelle speaks for the both of them. "We love you, but guys don't ever feel the *same way*. His game must be thick or that dick is."

"Nice try. I wish you could see how he is with me. Maybe then you'd get it. It just bothers me that I'd vibe with someone like this right before I leave for school."

"Because life would be boring if it didn't shake us up once in a while. Have your summer fling, keep him in rotation like I do my men, and for the love of God, send us a picture of this guy," Nya rages.

David's truck pulls in the driveway while Nya begs me to send the photo, and Michelle describes how her weekend went. He hops out of the truck with the engine running with the headlights on low. I flash my lights, and he staggers on the sidewalk toward the porch.

"Whatchu doing sitting out here?"

I point to the phone. "Gossiping with my girlfriends."

"About me, I hope."

Nya announces over the speaker, "We are!"

He blushes. "I don't wanna hold you from your friends. I made it home and noticed your hair tie was hanging on my gear shift. Thought you might need it."

"His gear shift!" Michelle and Nya laugh loudly.

"Girls, I gotta go. Call you tomorrow."

I lower the phone when he passes me the scrunchie, beaming at his ridiculousness. The look in my eyes invites him to kiss me. He lowers through the window, and we share a slow, sensual lip lock.

"Call me tomorrow when you get up."

I nod. "Okay."

He looks back at me before he hops in his truck.

I shout across the yard. "Ever heard of Smokey Robinson?!"

"Of course I have! Why?"

"I'll tell you later!"

The engine of his truck annoys the dogs nearby. They settle down the farther he exits the neighborhood, and I listen to it fade while feeling the very words Nya told me not to say erupt from my chest and burn my throat.

13

LOVE YOU A LITTLE BIT

DAVID

A revelation hits me over the head like a sack of nickels down in Nash. I'm in love with Maeva Martin. High on this feeling, I run to my dad and muster up the courage to ask if I can move into the guest house on the other side of the lake for a while.

His eyes twinkle when he realizes I'm in love. He and I both know it, because it's no rumor in my family that I loathe asking anyone, especially him, for anything. But Maeva humbles my pride and amuses my father.

"In the past, you wouldn't have asked. Hell, I'm surprised you asked at all. The David I know would have moved in there without permission and dealt with the wrath later." He stares me down until a patch of moisture forms on my forehead. "You want to use the guest house as a sex cave. Am I right, my boy?"

"Dad."

"I've seen her. And I get it, son. I was young once."

"You're still young, Dad."

"Yeah. Okay. Whatever. How's the band getting along?"

"We're good. I'm confident in saying we should get this deal in a few weeks. Then, I'll finally move out into a place of my own and get out of you and Mom's hair."

"We're not pushing you out, son. If things don't pan out the way you want them to, you know there's a spot for you and your brother in the company."

"It's going to work out for us." I take a deep sigh and look out of the window.

"I hope it does. Your dream is my dream. What I'm hoping you take from this conversation is why success is necessary for a man. A man has his own. If you had your own, you wouldn't be standing here at twenty-one, asking for my permission to lay with a woman in a place that doesn't belong to you. Do you see where I'm going here?"

I fume at the lecture. He regurgitates everything I already know, pointing out my age and the different path I chose to take in life. I've heard this speech over and over since I announced college wasn't for me.

"I knew where this conversation was going before I came to you. I was hoping, this time, it didn't take a nasty turn. Forget I even asked." I storm out.

He stops me at the door. "Has this girl seen your stubborn side yet, boy?"

I refuse to answer him.

"You can't go out into the world, making deals in any industry, if you're aren't willing to listen. I hope you remember my saying so if this audition goes well in a few weeks. In fact, call me so I can make sure you don't blow it."

I listen to him with a red face growing redder by the minute.

"And before you stomp out of here like a kid whose toy was snatched away, I was going to say, as your father, it wouldn't be right for me to outright give you permission to use the house to lay up with that young lady. However, I will turn a blind eye. But if your mother catches you, we never had this talk. Understood?"

Quickly, my eyes shift to him, and I nod with the most gracious smile.

"Like I said, I was young once." He pats me on my shoulder. "And don't fuck up. You know exactly what I mean by that."

I leave my father's office ashamed. Ashamed at how I acted, how he berated me, and that his words are true. I feel less than a man, not having my own place, and like he said, a kid still chasing a dream who hasn't found his success yet.

If it weren't inappropriate to tell him of the great time I had in the city with Maeva, I would have, with hopes he could help me understand what I didn't understand myself—this thing called love. But after the lashing he laid on me, I keep those feelings to myself.

♡

I SEE Maeva twice after I'm given the keys to the lake house. We settle for a quickie in the driver's seat of my truck each time to tide us over, though I'd last way longer if her ass pressed against the horn didn't kill my concentration.

She scooches on the seat to pull up her shorts. "Let's not make this a habit."

"I'm gonna make you eat those words come this weekend. I've been working on something for us between rehearsals."

"That's good to know. I was beginning to think the flame between us was fizzling out when I couldn't get in contact with you."

I place her hand on my chest. "I can assure you the flame is burning hot on my end."

By Sunday, Maeva is fed up with my disappearing act. I swing by her house to pick her up for dinner, and by force of habit, I kiss her when she opens the door.

"Ahem." Mrs. Martin clears her throat.

I let go of Maeva's lips, wrought with embarrassment, trying to wipe her lipstick from my mouth. "How you doin' this evening, ma'am?"

She scoffs and throws up her hands. "Nice of your folks to invite Maeva over for dinner again. I apologize I haven't had the time to do the same for you."

"No apology needed, ma'am. I'll be here with bells on whenever you say the word."

"Mm-hmm. Well, I have an early morning tomorrow. Maeva, be sure to lock up when you get in. You two be safe and enjoy your night." Mrs. Martin finally cracks a smile at me.

"Is Mr. Martin around? I wanted to tell him what I've been working on."

Maeva pushes me toward the door. "He's sleeping, babe. Let's go."

"Nice talkin' with ya, Mrs. Martin."

When the door shuts, Maeva plants a big one on me. "I couldn't wait to see you." Her eyes twirl staring into mine. "Tell me you've got us a hotel tonight."

I play it coy and pick up her featherweight body then throw her up against my shoulders. She playfully screams and kicks as I carry her to my truck and place her on the passenger side.

"Don't look now," she whispers. "We have an audience."

"Which house?"

Maeva chuckles. "Mine."

I help Maeva down and open the door for her. As I'm backing out of the driveway, I pretend not to notice Mrs. Martin staring at us from her bedroom window.

MY FAMILY PUTS on the usual airs when we arrive for dinner. After dessert, Mom steals Maeva away for a one-on-one in her garden while Dad, Moe, Amy, and I watch Sunday Night Football over a few beers.

The home team takes the lead near the half when Maeva and Mom come back inside. The look in Maeva's eyes concerns me.

I hold her hand. "We're gonna say good night."

Dad stands and shakes Maeva's hand with the same glimmer in his eyes he had during our conversation. "Good to see you again, Maeva."

"Why are you running off so soon?" Mom asks.

"Honey, let the kids be. You two have a good night."

"At least take some of this food with you," Mom insists.

We leave the house with another bag of leftovers. I stall on the porch. "There's something I want to show you." I lead Maeva behind the house. Her hands are clammy by the time we walk through the damp grass to reach the dock.

I step inside the canoe. "Take my hand."

She pulls away, holding the insulated bag like her purse. "It's dark. I'm not going out with you in the water this time of night." Her voice wavers.

"I won't let anything happen to you."

"Some things you can't control," she sasses.

I sigh and hand her a life vest. "Please, trust me. I really have something I want to show you."

From the look on her face, her mind doubts me, but her heart trusts me as she places her hand in mine and crosses into the canoe. Her eyes wander endlessly into the open darkness, and her shoulders shiver from the breeze.

"We won't be on the water long, but there's a blanket behind you if you need one."

Slowly, she turns to look behind her, hesitant to move a muscle.

"The boat's not going to capsize if you move around, sweetheart. It's safe to reach for it. I promise."

She looks at me with contempt in her glistening eyes, hating her choice to follow me on the water.

"We're almost there," I reassure her and row faster to the dock up ahead.

Maeva's chest finally decompresses when I throw the rope around the post, and relief erases the look of fear across her cute face. I assist her onto the boardwalk then lead her inside our love nest for the next few weeks.

"What is this place?"

"This is us." I take the bag of food from her hands.

She follows me into the kitchen. "Us?" Her forehead wrinkles.

"Our car chronicles have been amazing, but after our weekend in the city, I can't stand not being with you throughout the night."

"But how is this ours?"

"You let me worry about that." I grab both of her hands. "On the nights we don't want to be apart, this is our little slice of heaven—for now."

Maeva looks like a deer caught in headlights. I release her hands, confused by her reaction, afraid I've moved too fast.

I step back. "Or not?"

"Is the only way here by boat?"

"No. There's a road past my neighborhood that circles the lake to get here."

Her tiny feet pace the hardwood as she runs her fingers across the furniture. "Hmm. No dust. Does it come with a housekeeper?" She smiles at me.

"Yeah, me. I cleaned this place from top to bottom. I put new linens on the bed, stocked the fridge with juice and eggs, and filled the cabinets with liquor and snacks."

She opens the cupboards. "I don't know what to say, except you've outdone yourself."

"Maeva...I love you. I know you're going away and all, but I wanted to show you I will do anything to be with you. Have I made you happy?"

"You have." Her hands cross at her breasts. "You love me, huh?"

"I love the hell outta you, girl." I swing her around in my arms.

Her forehead presses on mine. "I love you too."

Finally, the words I've been waiting to hear.

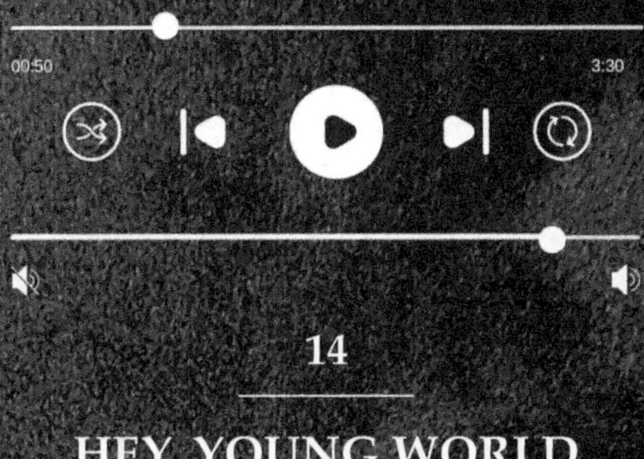

14

HEY, YOUNG WORLD

MAEVA

Song: "Hey, Young World" by Slick Rick

David's surprise earned him the right to have his way with me. Ideally, I would have tested the comfort of the bed and smelled the linens for freshness and thread count, but securing us a temporary nest... my need to perform an inspection went out of the window.

I lift my dress over my head in the den. David pounces on me before it hits the floor, initiating a fast play of passionate, wet, exasperated kisses. The backs of my thighs bump into the sofa, and he turns me around, bends me over the cushions, rips my panties to shreds, and inserts himself.

Long, pounding strokes withdraw a monotonous moan from my mouth. His fist wraps around my hair like a fingerless glove, and he drives my slick road like a madman with a death wish speeding in the rain. I feel naughty, desired, and dirty. I love it.

"That was quick."

He cuffs my cheeks. "I couldn't help myself. If you spend the night, I promise I'll make it up to you."

"Well, I rather much enjoyed that, being handled with—how should I say it—dominance."

"There's a lot I hope to learn about what you like." He pulls me closer and kisses the back of my shoulder.

"Well, with an offer like that, I'll stay the night."

Waking up with David's arm cradling my waist is undeniably fulfilling and addictive, especially after a beautiful, lascivious night.

Before dawn, I face my fears once more as David canoes us back to the other side of the lake and drives me home.

I waltz inside when a hint of orange and blue color the sky. Ma is in the kitchen, fixing breakfast, already dressed for work.

"I was beginning to think you forgot where you lived," she scolds me.

You knew she wasn't gonna be happy about you not coming home.

I stand at the door with my mouth open, catatonic with fear of her next choice of words, fearful my response will somehow be used further against me.

She raises her hand and shuts it closed, silencing me before I utter something idiotic. "You'll be happy to know I hired a nurse on Friday. With you heading off to school soon, there was no need to wait until the last minute."

"When do I meet him? Or her?"

"Today. He'll check in with you and your father around noon."

I nod, smart enough not to mention my plans to sleep all morning. No surprise to me, Ma delivers another jab before she heads out the door.

She judges me harshly with a cold once-over. "For someone who had a long night, you certainly look like it."

I pout and keep silent, holding in what David had done for me, which would prove we shared something real. I want to share it with her, but she is staring at me with her matronly *I know you better than you think* face and scoffs.

"Go get you some rest. Noon will be here before you know it."

(♡)

Nurse Devers arrives five minutes earlier than scheduled. My charcoal-covered face answers the door, surprised at how young he is. Dressed in sky-blue scrubs, white sneakers, and a clean, yellow baby face, he smiles and introduces himself.

"You must be Maeva."

"You're early. I mean, you must be Nurse Devers." I sway my hands for him to come inside.

He carries an oversized bookbag on his back as he passes through, snickering loud enough for me to hear.

"Sorry to interrupt your self-care time. You can call me Nick, by the way. It's nice to meet you." He reaches to shake my hand.

I meet him halfway and extend mine. "Okay, Nick. Nice to meet you as well. I'll go tell my dad you're here."

Passing the door to my room, I catch a glimpse of myself in the mirror. "Oh shit," I mumble, seeing the face mask hardened and cracked on my face. I tell Pop to make his way into the living room then rush to wash off the goo.

She thinks she is so smart.

Nick goes over his initial greeting of the client then goes outside to gather the rest of his gear from his car.

I giggle at my mother's strategy. "Pop, what are you and Ma up to?"

"This is all your mother's doing." He cracks up. "She raved on how well the boy is qualified."

"I thought you liked David?"

"I don't have a problem with the young man."

I grunt. "I should have been more proactive and selected a pretty, young female nurse for the job. See how she'd like it."

Pop laughs until he coughs. "You know good and well your

mother wasn't gonna go for that. The two of you sure keep me going."

"Well, this little plan of hers isn't going to work."

Pop taps my hand. "Be easy on your mother. She wants what's best for you, sweet pea. As do I."

Nurse Devers returns with an elastic band for Pop's first exercise.

"If I'm not needed here, I'm going to step away for a little while."

Nick looks at Pop. "I think we can take it from here."

I skip sleep, get dressed, and surprise my mother at her office. Her face wrinkles when I walk through the door.

"Why aren't you at the house?"

"Dad and Nick seem to be getting along just fine without me." I raise my brow at her. "I think he'll be a keeper."

She smiles, face filled with guilt. "You've assessed this in a few hours, have you?" She snickers. "He's quite a looker, that Nick."

"Very handsome, but not my type."

"What do you know about your type? You've had one boyfriend."

I sigh. "Why don't you like David?"

"Sweet pea, you're leaving for college soon. You are going to be amongst so many cute boys that you won't be thinking about David. And if being surrounded by cute boys, the wild parties, and the change of scenery doesn't come between you two, the distance will." She speaks with confidence.

I take a minute before my rebuttal. "Say you're right, Ma. Say we do break up. Why will that make you happy?"

She rises from her ergonomic chair and closes her office door. I hate the way she's looking at me as she joins me on the opposite guest chair facing her desk. It's the serious, *listen to me, I know what I'm talking about* look. The look of prophesying her life experiences onto me.

"I could never be happy seeing my daughter get her heart

broken. I've had more than one love in my life, Maeva. I know what it's like firsthand to be head over heels in love with a man many women adore—a musician, no less. Believe me when I say, multiple women will always be there in the cut, waiting for their shot. And sometimes they don't wait. They're proud to be second. Proud to be in the background of your ignorance and trust. Happy to be the bearer of your pain."

"Did you and his mother have a secret meeting or something?"

"I've never spoken to the woman. Why do you ask?"

"Because she said something similar to me last night."

"I knew you were holding something heavy when you came home. What did his mother say?"

"In her sweet and tactful way, she was swaying me to see our relationship as a friendship, encouraging me to be clear with David that we would always be friends and let him experience life on the road with a clear head. Then she threw in my face there would be loads of women he would entertain as the lead singer in a band."

"She's not wrong. I don't agree with her delivery, but I do agree with the message. You're both young and think you're in love, but life gets in the way, and love is only one part of a relationship. You'll see when you go off and actually live in the real world and have responsibilities, pay bills, manage your classes, your love life, money. The world looks different then."

Ma's face beams with a smug smile. She's been waiting to throw those darts at me, and they stick like thumb tacks on a cork board. They also hurt like hell.

❤

"Yes!" I shout internally close to midnight. Blood stains my sheets, and I breathe better than I have for a week.

The deepest exhale escapes my mouth. "Thank you, God," I

mumble, covering my head with the comforter, relieved I'm not in the family way. "I have to chill with the recklessness and tell him to strap up," I coach myself as I change the bed then hop in the shower.

By morning, severe cramps ruin the day David and I have planned together. We spend the afternoon snuggled in bed at our new oasis—napping, watching television, and relishing our ability to be alone without any boundaries.

He offers a pain-relieving back massage to ease the unbearable, contraction-mimicking spasms. I am spoiled and now feel the same way as him.

I could get used to this.

The week progresses, and so does the pain. I avoid him for days when the mood swings bring out the worst in me. By Thursday, David has had enough of the distance and shows up on my doorstep, posed with his elbow resting on the entrance, as if his thirty-second wait for me to answer the door is too long.

I resist the urge to jump in his arms when the truth is, I am happy he's here. "I thought we were on for tomorrow night after your gig?" I ask as I open the door.

He looks down at me and charms me with his baby blues. "I couldn't wait that long. Can we talk?"

My heart flutters at the words no one ever wants to hear. I welcome him inside, and his tracks stop at the door before it closes.

He glares into the living room. "Who are you?"

"I'm Nick. You are?"

"Fixin' to see my way out." David looks at me, breathing heavily. "Now I know why I haven't seen you."

Pop enters from his bedroom. "Hey, David. I missed you the other night. How's it going?"

"I thought it was going pretty great." David shrugs his shoulders.

"I see you've met the miracle worker taking over for Maeva when she leaves us next month?" Pop extends his hand.

David reaches for it and exhales deeply. "Ah, yeah?"

"They've met, Pop," I interrupt. "If you'll excuse us."

I lead David to the porch then let go of his hand to fold my arms. My eyes narrow in on him. He cuts me off before I can speak my mind.

"I—I—I thought..." he stammers.

"I know what you thought, but why?"

"You've been dodging me for days now. I know your friend was in town, but something felt off in my bones. Then I come here and see a guy in your house—I just got ahead of myself."

"Yeah, you did. I told you I get moody during my time."

"I know you did, but if I'm being honest, the last time I saw you, you were quiet. Like something else was on your mind."

"It was."

"Then don't keep me in the dark. I saw the look on your face when you and my mother came from outside."

"I don't want to talk about your mother."

"So it is her, then?"

I look away.

"Is it the house? Is it too much? Did I move too fast? Do something wrong? Please tell me. I miss you, girl." He reaches for my hand.

I reach for his, and he reels me in for a kiss. "The house is lovely. You haven't done anything wrong. I was in a bit of a funk this week. Trust me. You don't want to be around me when I'm crabby acting."

"I thought the back massage helped."

"It did, but you had rehearsals. I didn't expect you to lounge around all week and take care of me when you have your big audition coming up."

"It would have been lovely to come home to you afterward, though."

"You'll get your wish this weekend. How does that sound?"

"Like music to my ears."

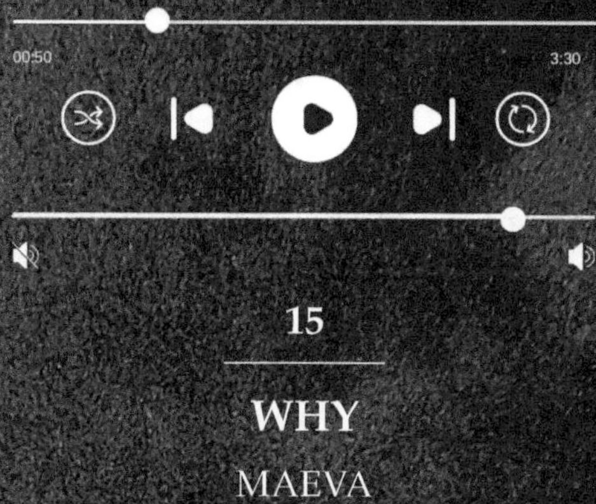

15

WHY

MAEVA

I'm nervous to see David when Friday arrives. His jealousy of Nick exposed a side to him I find unflattering and alarming. A possessiveness I've overlooked somehow. Is this what loving him will be like? Wild assumptions that cause him to fly off the handle? Claimed as property? Submission of myself in exchange for a connection more addictive than a drug?

I question my many feelings when I drive over to our haven. David meets me in the driveway, takes my bag, and greets me with a desperate, hungry kiss. I taste it on his lips, see it in his eyes, and feel it as he lingers on my face.

The intensity of being near him, and how he looks at me with the glimmer of the night sky in his blue eyes stings my chest.

"I was going to tell you something the other night, but you were so worked up the timing didn't feel right."

He smooches my forehead. "Tell me what?"

"I leave in two weeks."

The light in his eyes fades, and his grip around my waist falls feeble. My heart sinks at his forlorn face looking at me as if I've double-crossed him.

"Why? What changed?"

"We both knew I was leaving. It's just the way things worked out."

"What aren't you telling me?"

"Nothing. Going early will get me acclimated before classes, and I was offered to move in early to begin my work-study. I'm not keeping anything from you." I step back. "Besides, you're going to be busy after your big audition. You can focus on being the big rock star you are without having to worry about fitting me into your schedule."

"Maeva..."

"David. Let's enjoy the time we have left this summer before my nose is in a book, and you're on the road meeting new people and living it up with groupies and wild parties."

"Groupies and wild parties? Nonsense. Our time is being cut short because you're running away from me."

I raise my voice. "You act as if this isn't hard for me too. We met at the absolute wrong time in our lives."

"I disagree. I met you when I needed you most. Life isn't easy, but you roll with the punches."

"Men roll with the punches. Women have to plan, create, originate, innovate, or sacrifice by giving up themselves."

"Who's writing the songs here? You or me." He smiles to cut the tension between us, and our feet guide us back into each other's space. "I love you, Maeva. I don't want what we have to end."

I look up at him. "Just promise you won't let all the slutty girls make you forget how much you love me. I hear they get sluttier, prettier, and of a higher grade the more famous you become."

"That's the second time you mentioned other women. Is that what this is really about? Who's feeding you this garbage?"

I play with the neckline of his shirt. "I don't wanna argue."

He sighs. "Then what do you propose we do?"

"Just be."

His hands stroke my shoulders. "Can I kiss you now?"

He gazes into my eyes with the sexiest smirk I've ever seen on his kind face. For a moment, I become hopeful we'll survive the distance and forget about the cautionary tales his mother and mine warned me of.

Their fear and concern hold no weight when compared to his baby blues summoning me. My eyes smile at him, and my lips follow suit while I stand on the tip of my sneakers to receive the gentlest kiss David has ever laid on me.

"Now *this* is how I imagined it would be when I saw you today." He lifts my hand and twirls me around like we're on a dance floor. "What am I going to do with you?"

I lean forward and rest my head on his chest. "Keep on loving me, I suppose."

16

ON & OFF

DAVID

Maeva's news of an early split rattles me. She's pulling the rug out from under my feet, and it feels like being stabbed with a cold knife.

I bury the level of *pissedtivity* I feel from her betrayal deep down so I can enjoy her in every biblical way imaginable while searching for a way to convince her not to run away early.

She lifts her head from my chest and lodges the knife in my back further. "I got here late because I made a few stops." She reaches into her bag. "I took my first drive into the city to clear my head," she explains, pulling plastic bags from her duffel. "I went by Hattie's and bought the hot chicken we missed out on, and after our recent reckless behavior, I stopped by the drugstore and grabbed these."

She's arrived, sparing me little to no pain, twisting a box of condoms from side to side. The gesture drop-kicks me. She's already spoiled me with raw pleasure the last few times we were together, and now she's stripping me of her delicious fruit. The fruit I crave and long for on the nights I'm forced to spend alone. The fruit she has no way of knowing its sweetness. It's so good I dream about it every night and write songs thinking about it. The sweetness I've claimed as mine, because once you've tasted sugar at its finest, it's impossible to swallow shit.

I plaster a fake, ridiculous grin on my lips and stutter. "I... If... Um... If they're necessary for us to spend time together, you'll get no complaint from me." I cringe as I speak my biggest lie.

"Your eyes say something different." She chuckles. "Come on, let's eat."

She tosses the package on the sofa. The more I stare at them, the weirder the mood shifts between us. I feel like a stranger forcing conversation on her, so I shut up and let silence win.

Her lips smack on the sauce dripping from the sandwich. It's so quiet between us I hear her chew with her mouth closed.

We sit on opposite ends of the sofa with the box of condoms burning my sight. I turn on the TV then hand her the remote.

She pushes it away. "You pick," she says in the saddest tone that nearly kills me.

"I didn't plan on our evening being tense like this, Maev."

"I feared it would be once I told you I was...you know. Should I go?"

"Hell no. Why would you?"

"Because this awkwardness is my fault."

I move the box to the coffee table. "Come here."

Maeva sits on my lap and leans against me. I inhale her peachy fragrance and the spicy residue on her lips and hold her close.

"This is more like it." I kiss her saucy lips. "Sweet and spicy."

She studies my face. "How long do you plan on being upset with me?"

I steal another kiss. "I'm not mad at you. I'm mad at our situation."

Her head leans back. I give her the attention she wants and suck on her neck. She pants of pleasured bliss, then our eyes lock on each other, reading one another's minds, connecting on a deeper level.

What we share in our little love nest is coming to an end, and we both feel it without having to say.

The fear of losing one another and the sadness of the truth burns in her eyes and is felt in mine. I pick up the box and carry Maeva into the bedroom. She welcomes my pleasurable torture not once, but twice through the night, wrapping her legs around me and holding onto me like a trapeze gymnast who lost her swing.

When the roosters crow, a simple text shrinks my morning wood. Maev wakes me with light taps to my chest.

"Babe, I have to leave. My ma has been called in to work, and Nick is unavailable this morning. I'll come back later to pick up where we left off."

"God, I hate that guy." I groan and place my arm around her.

"What? You hate who?"

"Nick, the fucking prick."

She lifts my arm from around her waist and pokes me in the chest. My eyes open wide to a death stare and a pretty crumpled face.

"Why is Nick a prick?"

"What?" I sit up.

"You were talking out of your head just now. Why do you think Nick is a prick? What'd he do to you?"

"I saw how he looked at you."

"How can you want a long-distance relationship when you don't trust me?" Her tone chastises me.

"I do trust you. I don't trust him." I sweep my fingers against her legs. "Come lie next to me for a few more minutes. I didn't mean to—"

She cuts me off. "I need to get going. I'll call you later to see if we're still on for tonight."

"Why wouldn't we be?" I ask her as she throws on her clothes and walks out.

17

UNTIL YOU COME BACK TO ME

DAVID

Song: "Until You Come Back To Me" by Aretha Franklin

Ghosted. No call or text from Maev. Complete radio silence with my calls going to her voicemail sends me spiraling to solve the mystery of what's made her want to bail on me. Her cold side of the bed provides me with a glimpse of what it's going to be like if I lose her. Miserable.

The day ends with no word from her all day. It's Sunday. The day we always spend together. But all I hear are crickets outside my window.

The sun hides behind clouds from a storm covering the whole town, but I don't let the heavy rain stop me from finding myself at the top of Maeva's steps.

The vein in my neck tightens when Nick's face greets me at the door. The sight of him refreshes the spat Maev and I had before she left our special place, but when he calls her name, my buried anger rises and travels to my fist balled up against my thigh.

I cringe when I hear Maeva say his name, but I hate it even more hearing hers flow from his lips. It makes me think of how he gazed at her when he thought I wasn't looking on the day we were introduced.

Let it go. Don't let him be the reason you push her away. Control your temper, dumbass.

"Is that David?" Mr. Martin shouts from the living room.

"Yes, sir." I push the door open wider so he can see me.

"It's nasty out there. Come on in."

I walk past Nick.

"How've you been?" I ask her father, closing the door behind me.

He shakes my hand. "Doing pretty alright, son. How about yourself?"

"Everything's good." I sneak a look around. "Sorry to drop by unannounced."

"No need for that. Maeva's in her room. Go on back. Second door on the right. But do me a solid and keep it open for me, son." He nods, pointing down the hallway.

"Yes, sir." I glaze over Nick packing up his equipment with a smirk on my face.

Maeva's room looks somewhat how I pictured it. Deep-purple painted walls, white furniture with bright pops of fuchsia here and there, and homemade shelves with the tiny pieces of furniture she constructed.

She sits up on her bed when I stand at her door. My brows lift, waiting for her permission to step inside. She grins on the side of her mouth and removes her headphones. I take a step forward and pause until she gives me clearance to enter.

"I came to say I'm sorry. And admit I'm jealous. And to tell you that I trust you."

Maeva tilts her head and stares at me.

"With you not taking my calls, I went up to the main house and had a chance to speak with my mother. Why didn't you tell me what she said to you?"

"Because she's your mother. Who am I to think you'd take my

word over hers? Besides, she was nice about it. I guess. At least I think she meant well."

"She had no right to say those things to you. She can't speak on things she doesn't know or on my behalf. How could she possibly know what I feel?"

"Take it easy on her. She was protecting me for the day you and I both know is coming. We both feel it. That's why yesterday was so strange."

"So what, we had an off day. Don't let my mother get into your head."

"I could say the same about *you know who*." She points toward the front of the house.

"Touché." I kiss her while swallowing my pride.

"I'm terrified everything she said will come true."

I lift her chin. "Nobody has all the answers, and I'm not giving up on us. I love you. I hope that counts for something."

"It counts for everything." Her fingers cup my face. "How about we forget about this fight and focus on us after you sign those dotted lines."

"And this is why I know you're the one for me." I kiss her once more then jump at the slamming sound of a car door.

"Ma's back from the store. We better go up front before she cuts off your good friend and has you singing as a soprano."

18

STAY WILD

DAVID

Between missed phone calls and Maeva preparing to leave, time proved itself to be my enemy. I was headed to the city, about to be posted up in a hotel room with the likes of the guys and a fully loaded clip. Far from appealing.

I refuse to go to the audition without seeing her, so I re-route the van to her side of town for a kiss from my good luck charm. The band fumes, but I don't give two shits.

"This guy," Souse complains.

"I've done everything you guys asked of me this week, and my lady hasn't complained once. All I need is five minutes with her, dammit!"

"Chill." Moe punches Souse in the arm. "Five minutes, bro. Is that all it takes?"

The band snickers.

Maeva's eyes glisten the moment she steps on the porch. I turn around and give the guys a look so evil they know to mind their manners.

Lim and Moe shout from the truck. "Hey, Maev!"

She waves to the band. "I wasn't expecting to see you until you had news." Her shoulders slump shyly in front of the guys.

"I couldn't go without seeing you first. I'm ready for it to be over and done with so I can get back to you and pick up where we left off." I sneak in a smooch. "You know we never got around to making up after our fight."

She smiles bigger than a serial scratcher finally winning the lottery, waning me with inviting eyes. "I know. So go claim your dream and hurry up and come home."

I hold her in my arms. "That's why I'm here." I cover her with my back turned to the guys and kiss the sweetest lips I've been missing for days. "To kiss my good luck charm."

"This is your moment."

"Baby, do me a favor. Wait for me at the house tomorrow."

"If that's what you want."

"It is." I bottle up a few more kisses. "Love you."

"Love you too."

The guys resort to the normal tomfoolery, teasing me with kissing noises as I trek back to the van. We hit the highway, enter the city, and check into a rinky-dink motel Lim reserved until it's time for our performance.

The four of us pack inside one room with double beds, secluded from the world until showtime. When we get the call, a multitude of energies and emotions run rampant between us. The looks on the guys' faces are a mix of fear, nervousness, and determination.

"This is it," Moe says.

Souse riles us up, clapping his hands. "Time to prove ourselves."

We take center stage where the bright, off-white lanterns hanging from the ceiling units wake us up from the simulation of dreams we were cast in. Moe nods and breaks the first smile. I relax and view the execs as no different from the people we play for in the dives and hole-in-the-wall bars on our side of town.

Moe taps the rim of his drums, and I exhale a long breath, following his lead to set us off for the best performance of our career.

✻

Post the audition, my nerves decide to make an appearance while Souse rants, pacing around the room like a hyper kid.

"We've come too far to fail and walk away without getting this deal."

Moe silences him a few times as we wait like sitting ducks for the execs of the label to make their way to us backstage. With Souse creating anxious energy around us, we take turns circling the small box, wall to wall. Praying. Wishing. Hoping they'll walk through the door and tell us we finally have a label behind us.

Twenty minutes pass, and Moe blurts, "Fuck this! They should have come running in here after the way we lit this house on fire!"

Souse pats his back. "I'm giving them five more minutes, and then I'm goin' lookin' for 'em."

"I'm sure they're deliberating and discussing their approach," Lim adds.

"You say that, yet all of the fruity-tootie bands are getting signed," Moe argues.

"We got this!" Lim silences the room.

"Yeah, well if so, what's our plan of attack?" Souse asks.

"Our old man said for us to call him to hammer out the paperwork if need be," Moe tells them. "It's his way of saying not to sign anything without legal present."

The guys laugh for the first time since we wrapped our set. The McCloud brother duo knocks on the door, then lets themselves in, followed by two women half their age and tempting on the eyes.

"Great show, fellas," says Palmer, the youngest of the two.

"Excellent show." Jamison, the elder brother, goes around the room and shakes all of our hands.

"Gentlemen, don't tell us to shove off after we've waited back here for half an hour," says Moe.

Our eyes shift toward my big brother beating his chest.

"Is he your spokesperson?" Palmer asks.

"No," we answer in unison.

"Well, I like his gumption. And he's right. We shouldn't have made you wait this long to tell you we want you on the label."

Collective sighs, yesses, and applauds occupy our dressing room. In a state of shock, I bury my face in my hands, holding back tears of joy.

"You hear that, boys. We fucking rocked!"

"That you boys did indeed. My brother and I have family in the area and will be in town until Sunday. Expect a call from my secretary to arrange a time where we'll meet and hammer out the details of both our visions." Palmer points to the prettiest woman of the two standing behind him.

Jamison cut in. "I think you boys will be happy with what we have in mind. I say we fly you and your families to Manhattan, show you how you'll be living in the city, and all the bells and whistles in our studio where you'll begin cutting your album."

I chime in. "There are studios here."

"Yeah, but they're not ours. Here's hoping we can come to an agreement and start working on that number one debut."

Palmer's secretary hands him a bottle of bubbly. He pops the cork. His secretary and the other woman shriek as it pierces the wall, and the champagne fizzles down the sides.

"Red cups okay?" Souse holds up his cup below the bottle, catching the drip.

The brothers laugh.

"As long as it goes down smooth, I don't care what it's poured in," Palmer says while his secretary empties a traveling case of glasses.

Souse gives her a once-over and winks at her. "I like how you travel."

She smiles then issues each of us a flute. "Would you like for me to pour, Mr. McCloud?"

Palmer grins and nods then shifts his eyes between us. "This is the type of service you can expect being on our team. Cheers."

As the champagne flows, our tiny backstage box echoes with shouts, hollers, and childhood chants. The McCloud brothers excuse themselves while we stay behind and empty the bottle.

Souse becomes boisterous. "Where are we going to celebrate boys?"

Lim stands on the edge of a chair. "It doesn't matter! We're fucking rock stars baby! Let's hit the strip!"

Liquor calls to our high, and word gets out we're popping bottles at Brown's. It doesn't take long for a crowd to fall in and join the party without knowing the cause for celebration.

I find myself a free moment and step out back to call Maeva. "We got it!" I say as soon as she answers.

"I knew you would. How do you feel?"

"Come down here and let me show you."

"That good, huh?" She laughs.

"I honestly don't have the words."

"Ineffable."

I press the phone tighter to my ear. "Who's not fuckable?"

"What? Um, never mind. I can tell you're smiling through the phone, so I have a pretty good idea how happy you are right now."

"I almost cried. I still might. I'm way past cloud nine, baby."

"I'm happy for you. And the guys. Where are they?"

"Inside, celebrating. I'm serious about you coming down tonight. I'll get us a room."

"I would love to, but it's late, and this is your moment with the band. I don't want to make them like me any less by interrupting your big night. I'll be at the house tomorrow like you asked. Okay?"

I sigh as a knot forms in my chest. "It is late. That was insensitive of me. I just wish you were here."

"I'll be there for the next big moment."

"You know I'm going to hold you to that. Right?"

"Yes. I know. Now go have a good time. And congratulations."

I do what Maev says—have a good time. Some would say a great time. The fellas and I party hard with familiars and strangers alike, dancing with girls on tables, throwing cash to naked women in strip clubs, and bar hop 'til everything shuts down and the golden light in the sky shows us we've survived to live another day.

A few biscuits tie us over 'til we pass out in the room, faded out of our minds, and sleeping off the brew stench leaking from our pores. By the time I wake up, Lim's hanging halfway from the desk chair with his hands cradling his head. Moe lies beside me, snoring like a bear, with his arms wrapped around me, and Souse is walking into the room.

"Who knew you lames were featherweights? You slept through the housekeeper and manager banging on the door. But no worries. I paid for an extra night to keep them from calling the law on us."

"Not a good start, boys," I mumble.

"What time is it?" Lim groans.

"Supper time."

I lift my head. "Say again?"

"Quarter past six. You boys were out like a lighthouse in a hurricane."

I jump up from the bed. "Shit!"

I'm beside myself, raising pure cane and hell with the guys to get their asses up and in the van. The blame shifts from one to the other as we pack up, talk shit, and pile in.

In a rage, I skid out of the lot. "What exactly happened last night?"

"If anyone remembers, please tell me. I might want to journal about it." Moe snickers under his breath.

"Journal," Lim repeats him over chuckles.

"We had a ball, like in the good old days, is what happened," Souse brags then scuffles my hair. "This one stopped acting like he was a househusband on a leash and let loose."

I swat his hand off me. "Thank God no girls came back to the room with us."

"No girls came back with you, but you ain't so innocent. That filly you were tonguing down on that table would have come with us if her boyfriend hadn't started that ruckus. Whew! I tell ya, the girls are gonna be way easier to get from here on out."

My eyes study the road ahead as I shuffle faces in my memory. I scramble to picture a girl I allegedly kissed. My pits begin to seep sweat through my t-shirt as I wrestle with the notion of what can't be true. None of what Souse says rings a bell.

I scream out loud, banging on the steering wheel. "This is not how I wanted this to go! I don't remember kissing any girl, Souse. Fuck!"

"Calm down, beau. I wouldn't have let anything go down," Moe assures me.

"Did anyone film us? Man! I'm fucked!"

Souse kisses his teeth and lowers his hat over his eyes. "I told you not to get serious."

I pull over to the side of the road. "Get out!"

"Fuck off! I'm keeping my ass in this seat."

I shove Souse on his forehead. "I swear if you say anything about my girl, I'm gonna knock you on your ass!"

"The only reason I won't pop you back is that pretty mouth of yours is my ticket out of here, so go ahead and hit me. I can take it."

Moe cuts in. "Okay, everybody chill the fuck out! No one is

popping anyone! Bro, I've got your back. I wouldn't have let anything scandalous happen last night. I like Maeva. Hell, I like *you* with her. And Souse, get over yourself and stay out of my brother's business. Let's get home, get out of these rank-ass clothes, and get our heads back in the game."

I merge back onto the highway and dial Maeva's number. No answer. Three calls go unanswered, and the sweat from my arms is now bleeding through my shirt. The truck fills with silence while I speed like a maniac to the exit and pause when the light turns green.

"It's green," Lim points out.

"I see that," I say, turning left toward Maeva's house.

I pull in front of her driveway, and a dose of my own medicine is served to me fresh and hot.

19

PICK UP YOUR FEELINGS

DAVID

Song: "Pick Up Your Feelings" by Jazmine Sullivan

The silence in the van grows thicker as my face turns red, and the sound of me gulping air gorges down my throat. The fellas begin asking questions, but I ignore their prying and conceal my anger before I hop out of the truck.

My heart falls to my stomach, turning like a twister setting foot on the ground to do damage. My steps are slow as I approach Maeva sitting on the porch next to Nick's smug face and evil brows taunting me.

One good punch is all I need.

He snidely says, "I hear I should ask for your autograph while I have the chance."

"Is that what you heard?" I answer him with my eyes glued on Maeva.

"Maeva says you…"

I face him. "You mind if I have a word with my lady in private?"

Nick gets up and glances at me over his shoulder then closes the door after peeking at Maeva. A sharp exhale slips from my mouth as I struggle to hide my anger behind a blank face.

Maeva refuses to look at me. I call her name. She avoids revealing the fury in her eyes to me. Her usual smile is buried beneath disappointment and ridicule, but she's still the most stunning woman I've ever laid eyes on. Angry and all, I can't resist seeing the beauty in her flaming cheeks and pouty mouth.

"Baby, I…"

Slowly, she looks me up and down. "Baby." She scoffs. "You look like you enjoyed yourself last night."

She crosses her arms and purses her lips. Her nostrils spread, and she turns a pastel shade of red while her eyes yell at me to *GET THE FUCK OFF MY PORCH!*

I step forward to kiss her. She leans back. The scrunched expression on her face feels like a punch to the gut.

"You can't be serious right now." Her eyes roll at me while sucking her teeth through a curve on the side of her mouth. "You show up late, smelling and looking like last night's garbage, and expect me to melt in your arms?"

"I…I'm…I fucked up. I'm stank, wretched, late, and hungover at your door, hoping you'll forgive me. I never meant for my big night to turn out like this."

She lowers her eyes to my feet. "I told you this would happen."

I run my hands over my face. "This was one time. Baby, you know I have to kiss you whenever I see you. Can I?"

Her cheeks rise as she sighs. "Only because I don't want to embarrass you in front of your friends. But we need to talk."

Moe shouts from the van. "Maeva, it's my fault! Don't give him too much hell!"

She plasters on a fake smile and waves to my brother. "Okay, Moe! Congratulations, by the way!" She continues to smile when she faces me.

"What do I have to do to make this up to you? I'll do anything."

"There's nothing you can do. Don't you see? This is how it's gonna be now that you've got your deal. This sort of thing will be full-time, and you don't need a girlfriend holding you back from enjoying it. And I personally don't enjoy sitting around mad because you didn't check in, or show up, or keep your word when I kept mine."

"Maev, you know I would never intentionally let you down. Time got the best of me."

"Apparently, alcohol got the best of you too. It's seeping through your pores."

The look of disgust in her eyes and the brusqueness in her voice slices me into tiny pieces. And though I deserve her brash words and cold demeanor, it hurts like a motherfucker, and her delivery cuts the high I was riding hours ago to shreds.

"David, I'm proud of you, and I'm glad you're okay. You went after your dream and are about to live a life most will envy. We had a great summer. Now, it's over."

"You're not the only one in this relationship. I have a say, and it's not. I wanted to celebrate last night with you. I still do. I'm gonna go clean up, come back to pick you up, and we can finish having this discussion then."

"Just call me once you're settled in. I'll drive myself over."

"Whatever you say. I know I'm in no position to call the shots."

She looks at me unamused. I feel her anger, her hurt, and her uncertainty travel into my chest through the bridge that connected us the night we met. A cold sweat forms across my forehead as I fear the woman I love has closed her heart to me.

She leaves me standing on the porch with my tail tucked between my legs—dismissed without our normal insatiable kiss goodbye and lingering gaze into each other's eyes.

In disbelief, I pick up my feelings and dawdle down the sidewalk backward to the van, hoping to catch a glimpse of her staring at me from her window. But all I see are closed curtains and a closed door.

Moe sticks his head out of the window. "How bad did she hurt you, Cowboy?"

The guys snicker loud enough for me to hear, unconcerned and unaware of just how bad I'm feeling in my chest.

"I think she just put me on notice."

Fuck. I'm in the doghouse, about to get my walking papers. And she never did give me that kiss.

HIGH & DRY

MAEVA

Song: "High & Dry" by Bilal

I drive to the lake house, recounting how I felt waiting for David to show up.

- 11 a.m., I was angry.
- Noon, livid.
- 2 p.m., worried.
- And 4 p.m., done.

My feet press the gas then ease up every few seconds. I'm wrestling with making him wait for me and never showing up. Be the tit for his tat. Yet the wheels continue on the path to get to him, and I'm pissed with myself.

David has given me a firsthand account of what life will be like with fame at his heels. Late-night partying, broken promises, and wrinkled lines on my forehead. He's also proved both of our mothers right. A sting that burns like a match struck on my skin. That burn will leave a mark but not as deep as the one of him letting me down.

I hate feeling anger toward him, just as much as I loathe not driving into the city like he asked me to. I even contemplate placing the blame for his actions on myself so he can truly be happy with his accomplishment by the time I park my car on the rocks.

He comes outside and opens my car door, holding a bouquet of yellow roses. "Don't break up with me."

My shoulders slump, and I bite my tongue. "Can we go inside and talk?"

He helps me out of the car and exhales when he sees my overnight bag in the backseat. My chest tightens from the touch of his fingers stroking my arm as we walk inside the house. He throws my bag on the sofa. I throw my purse next to it.

David withers away into the bedroom. I press on his heels, and he turns around quick-fast and clobbers me with a hard kiss.

"Maev, I fucked up." He tosses the roses on the bed and squeezes me tight as a bear hug.

"I'm not mad at you anymore."

"But you said we need to talk."

"Because we do. I don't want this big moment to be ruined by us having an argument. When I said we need to talk, I was going to propose we slow things down and be friends with benefits. That way, there's no pressure to keep tabs on each other with the distance, and we'd respect where we both are in life without the hassle of titles or commitment."

"No. I don't wanna be your friend. I'm your fuckin' man! I want you, Maeva!"

"And I want you! But I know I'll get hurt, and I hate how I'm feeling right now! I don't wanna be mad at you! But I am!"

David consoles me. "Baby, I'm sorry. I don't ever wanna hurt you. I love you so much."

Heat begins to blaze in my body from his touch. I push him away. David forces me in his arms and strokes the center of my back until I wilt in his embrace.

"David, I'm scared. I'm excited to experience life away from my parents, but I wanna stay here with you too. I'm angry about this morning, but I'm happy for you also. I have so many conflicting feelings going on inside of me I fear I'm gonna explode."

"I knew you were holding back. Anything else you not telling me?"

"Yes. I'm in love with a man who is gonna break my heart, and he doesn't even know it."

I said it. I've spoken my truth. Revealed why I am being distant. Confessed I am head over heels in love with a rising rock star and am not as tough as I've been pretending.

David lifts me in the air. "I was beginning to think you changed your mind about me."

I finally allow his sumptuous lips sway me into surrender. "This frightens me."

"It frightens me too. But I ain't scared to fight for what I want."

21

THIS FEELING

DAVID

Song: "This Feeling" by Alabama Shakes

My baby affords me the luxury to hold her in my arms. I cling to her as if it's the last time I'll be afforded to do so after her silly suggestion of being friends with benefits. I could never just be her friend. And I'll never be okay seeing her in the company of another man.

We make our way to the bed, where I brush the sides of her face with the back of my finger. I watch her release her anger with her eyes closed, and I vow to myself to never make her feel like she comes second ever again.

I whisper in her ear, "I don't want us to be over." I lift her just as easily as my guitar and sit on the bed, placing her in my lap. "I have something for you."

She smiles at me. "I bet you do."

My finger slips in her shorts and parts her thighs.

"Ah," she moans.

Like the cramped space of a glove, my fingers fit snug and tight in her wetness, preventing me from maneuvering my fist inside, and her shorts rip at the seam.

"Fuck 'em. You can buy me another pair."

I grip on her outer thighs and lift her to slide down my cock.

Her body moves up and down on me. "David," she sighs.

"Fuck, baby, when you call my name like that, I...you feel so damn good."

She moans aloud from the splendor of my manliness, controlling how and where she wants to move. Shame engulfs me as I can't hold back. It's been too long since we've fucked, and in her bare walls, I don't stand a chance.

"Can I get one now and another one later?"

"You better," she says, welcoming my lifeblood inside of her.

I release a heavy load as she clenches her pussy around my dick, grunting in shame from the record time it took for her to milk me. Her warm walls grip me like they don't want to let me go. It boosts my ego to know she enjoys me that much.

"We might should fight more often."

She chuckles.

"I'm teasing. But damn, girl." I bite on her lip. "I missed the hell outta you."

"So much for the box in the other room."

"I couldn't help myself."

"Neither could I."

Later came sooner than we thought. We go at it like rabbits after a brief intermission of Maeva feeding us cold fries and stepping out of the bathroom naked.

Man, what a sight to see.

I take us into the silent night. No sound of the television. No sound of passing cars. Just the two of us, breathing heavy, exchanging moans and groans, and her looking into my eyes when she comes, making me feel like a man by making her feel like a woman.

Around 2 a.m., she sits up against the headboard with curled brows, staring at me. "Whatcha doing?"

I'm at the foot of the bed with my guitar in hand. "I told you I had something for you."

"Apparently, you had two things for me." She grins.

I strike the first chord, shaking off the nerves from her undivided attention. "I finally finished your song."

"My song?" Her cheeks flush red.

"You're the first to hear it. Tell me what you think. Okay?"

She nods, covering her mouth.

I fumble with the chords until I tune to D-flat. For the first time in a long while, my nerves shiver. Jitters I haven't felt since my final high school talent show. And here they are, out of the blue, stirring and instigating my first private performance for the love of my life.

> *Wild hair tight jeans*
> *Face of a goddess queen*
> *This girl's the one in my dreams*
> *I now know what love means*
> *Let me say it again*
> *Wild hair tight jeans*
> *Face of a goddess queen*
> *This girl's the one in my dreams*
> *I now know what love means*
> *I was up on my luck to get you*
> *Baby you know it's true*
> *I come alive when I'm witchu*
> *And that's why—I can't quit you*
> *I'll wait if I have to*
> *When you fall, I'll catch you*
> *Loosing you I just can't do*
> *You can quit me, but I cannot quit you*
> *I can't quit you.*

Maeva hops from the bed and runs into the front room. I sit

confused and embarrassed, wondering if the song is too much or if she hates it. I don't know whether to go after her or sit still like a duck.

I lay my strings on the bed when she reappears. She stands in front of me with teary eyes.

"Baby, what's wrong? Was I wrong to write..."

She places her finger over my mouth. "It was beautiful."

"Then why'd you run out?"

"To prepare myself."

"For what?"

Maeva leans down to kiss me. Her gentle lips serenade me with a song of her own as her hand massages my cock. I'm ready to strike a third time, struggling to demonstrate composure every passing second I'm not inside of her.

My shoulders straighten as my core shudders from her handy work. I talk to myself as my heart rate increases and my breath shortens.

Her tone of voice lowers to alto. "You like this?"

"Yes."

Her eyes hold mine, and I change my position while staring into them.

How can I be mad at her for leaving to follow her dream?

I turn into a simp while in her hands, literally. The careful precision she is stroking me, rolling her hands around my shaft like dice, is hypnotizing me to her spell. Then she...

Mercy, mercy me.

Maeva keeps her eyes on me as she falls to her knees, breaking our gaze when she places her pretty lips around the tip of my cock. She licks it like a cone melting in the sun. The words *marry me* nearly escape my mouth as I jerk and lean back, calling her name.

"Maeva," I whisper, praying to the Almighty for mercy and restraint not to propose.

She pauses her swirling tongue. "Tell me how you want me to suck it."

"Jesus Christ," I mumble, hearing such vile words come from her mouth. "However you do it, baby, is fine with me." I roll my neck upward and inhale when I smile at her.

She opens her mouth wide and kisses my bell end with her tonsils. I gasp for air and shiver in her mouth, fighting the urge to pull her hair and guide her to my hedonistic erogenous zone.

Do it. She might like it. Tell her how you imagined this moment and how you want her mouth around the head while grinding you with her hands. No. It's too soon. Don't ruin it. Just enjoy it.

The look in her eyes while working on me sends me into space. I don't blink, in fear I'll miss one second of this blessing. My inner voice quiets as Maeva slows her suction and pleasures me sensuously. Innocently. Warily.

I'm barely holding myself together and blossom fuller in her mouth.

She senses the difference and lifts up. "How was that?"

Unapologetically, I throw her on the bed and pounce on her like a lion on a gazelle. Her moans bring out the animal in me, and the thought of her leaving me evokes a mad, hidden beast settled deep in my bones.

I can't make love to her with the level of excitement and lust flowing through my veins. I fuck her like she's being punished, and in a twisted way, she is. I fuck her like she's stolen something from me, which she has. My heart. I fuck her like she needs— fast, strong, deep, and so good she'll have no choice but to think of me when she leaves or dares to lie with another.

My name and my face will always cross her mind when she feels the urge to succumb to desire. Me. David Boyd. Her one true love.

22

TIME

MAEVA

Song: "Time" by Culture Club

I watch a spider in the corner of the window swing on its web. Normally, I'd kill it out of fear that I'll wake up and find it's made its way closer to me, but this morning, I'll spare its life, as there's already a tragic ending happening in the room.

While David sleeps, I quietly cry, listening for the wheezing sound he makes when he's out cold. My tears drip on the pillowcase while I'm caged in his arms. One by one, they fall while I'm up thinking about the sweet lyrics in his song, knowing they'll live on forever...when we won't.

I cry for our love. I cry because I know distance will kill it. I cry because what we have is clouding my judgment and making me second-guess the plans I had before we met. I cry because I'm willing to do whatever he asks, and it frightens me.

I lie here, loathing time. The main obstacle proven to be our enemy, bringing us together to only break us apart as we're in different phases in life, and introducing me to the greatest love I'll never get out of my system then ripping it away from me like it means nothing.

The hiss rattles from his mouth for five minutes straight, and I slip from his hold. I leave my torn shorts on the dresser and throw on the sweats from my bag.

For a few minutes, I watch him sleep and press my luck, kissing his chest one last time. Then I place the letter I wrote for him between the strings of his guitar and leave before the sun brightens the darkness shrouding me.

23

WHERE IS MY MIND

DAVID

Song: "Where Is My Mind" by Pixies

My instincts were right. Maeva handed me walking papers, and I'm far from present, sitting in this meeting with the McClouds. It's hard to focus on the deal, having lost the best thing to happen to me.

The words in her note have left me disheveled and despondent, and I'm grateful my father and the family attorney have stepped in as our agents to sort out the details of the contract. But I need them to hurry up so I can go over to Maeva's and plead with her to change her mind. Our time together was indeed expiring, but our passion was far from dying. Far from over.

The eldest McCloud brother requests I remove my sunglasses. I do so without a problem to assure them they aren't getting into cahoots with an addict and wasting everyone's time.

"Son, is there a reason you look glum? This is what you've been waiting for."

"I'm ecstatic."

"Can't tell from lookin' at ya."

I throw them off with a lie. "I thought when we got here I'd be more lax. Now my mind is focused on not fuckin' it up."

They buy my bullshit, and I continue to sit quietly and not crack a smile until the photographers snap shots of us signing our John Hancocks. The image of the moment I achieved my dream and lost my girl. What are the odds?

We wrap things up in my father's office, and I'm set to jet out and win my woman back. Mom, alongside close friends and family, surprise us with a collective congratulations when we open the door, and I'm stuck putting on airs and a fake smile for another hour, crumbling inside, compressing my torment while everyone else gets tipsy and celebrates—doing what I should be.

When the pain is no longer easy to hide, I sneak out of my own party and head over to the Martins'. Maeva's mother welcomes me inside. Her face no longer appears pretentious or spiteful. Her brows aren't raised for once, and an almost smile is nearly formed on the side of her mouth.

"David!" I'm addressed with interest by Mr. Martin.

"How you doin', sir?"

"What brings you by?" Mrs. Martin asks.

"I notice Maeva's car is not out front. May I chat with you two until she gets back?"

She and Mr. Martin look at each other.

"Have you eaten?" Her mother's brow rises.

"Oddly enough, no, ma'am. I've been around food all evening and haven't had a bite."

She waves at me to cross into the house. "Have a seat at the table. I was just about to fix Mr. Martin a plate, and I owe you a dinner."

Truth is, I haven't had an appetite all day, but if stuffing myself with Mrs. Martin's late offer gets her to take a liking to me, I'll swallow whatever she puts on my plate.

"How *you* been getting along, young man?" Mr. Martin asks me.

I exhale ruefully. "Not too good if I'm being honest."

"I hear you're about to be a big deal. I assumed you'd be over the moon."

"Yeah, we finalized the deal this afternoon. I'm happy about it, but I wish Maeva was here to celebrate it with me. She hasn't taken my calls all day. Any idea where she might be?"

Mrs. Martin places a hefty plate in front of me with smothered chicken over rice, whipped potatoes, and cinnamon apples that put my mother's food to shame. One whiff, my loss of appetite becomes a thing of the past, and my fork sparks as I dig in.

The Martins look on in silence at my antics. When I realize I'm making a spectacle of myself, I apologize.

"Pardon me."

"No, go right ahead." Mr. Martin smiles. "My wife loves it when people enjoy her cooking."

"She and my mother have that in common. But don't tell her I said this is the best meal I've ever had. I wish you would have invited me over for dinner sooner."

"Thank you." Mrs. Martin smiles. "You can always stop by for a plate. That is, whenever you're in town. Are you excited to be hitting the road?"

"I'm still taking everything in. This weirdness between me and Maev kind of blindsided me."

Mrs. Martin sighs heavily and nods to Maeva's old man. He clears his throat and knocks my heart out of my chest, revealing that Maeva skipped town hours after she left me passed out from a night of passion imprinted on my brain.

She was half-packed by the time I rolled up on her and Nick sitting on the porch, and if it weren't for the long meeting and party at my folk's house, I would have caught her two hours ago before she left.

"Was she waiting on me?" I ask.

The Martins ignore my question.

"Why'd she leave so early?"

"Didn't she tell you? Her friend is moving into an apartment at Bowie State. Maeva is gonna stop by her new place and take her time driving to Rochester."

I shake my head no. My heart is broken, and I feel lost with no one to turn to that will understand how deeply I feel for this woman. I'm surrounded by people throwing our age, timing, and career into the equation of why we shouldn't be together. But they're all wrong. When a man knows, he knows, and the one girl I want to go through life with has let the naysayers push her away from me.

Mrs. Martin offers me comfort. "It was easier for her this way. You'll be occupied, and she gets to settle in early."

"I'm too late." I drop my head. "Thanks for dinner. I should get going."

Mr. Martin extends his hand. "I'll be looking for you on those award shows. You take it easy, and congratulations, David."

24

SPIDERWEBS

MAEVA

Song: "Spiderwebs" by No Doubt

You'd think my mother has a crystal ball showing her how we'd play out. All it took was the first celebration of David's achievement to show me how things would quickly turn—in his favor, not mine.

So, cutting ties with him abruptly is what I'll do. Cold turkey. That's how I'll leave him. Quick and stealth-like in the early morning light.

The words in his song make me unsure of myself, have me questioning my own mind. While listening to him sing about me, my heart breaks, and I cry internally. Another hour with him and I'm likely to change my plans to revolve around his. It's scary to think I'd betray myself, my dreams, and my future for a guy I've known for a month. And what's scarier is that I'm convinced he's worth my doing so. Worth centering my life around him, all for love.

I kiss him in his sleep, hurry home to hug my parents good-bye, and hit the road. For hours, I pretend I'm strong, avoiding his texts then blocking him completely so I won't see any notifications or his name.

By nightfall, I reach Nya's apartment, happy to stretch my legs and cry on her shoulder. Her remedy for my sorrow: giving me a tour of her campus and hunting for cute boys to keep us company during my visit.

The men at Bowie are striking, handsome, and familiar. Dark gods with smooth brown skin. Olive-toned gentlemen with buff arms and chiseled jawlines. Curly haired yellow cuties with almond eyes and peach fuzz above their lips.

It's clear why Nya wanted an apartment off campus: to avoid her mother's rules during the summer, live freely in her own space, and host booty calls as she desires.

The temptation is there. But so is the competition. Like normal, women outnumber the men everywhere you go, but Nya's ample ass cheeks make her the pick of the litter.

She introduces me to a dashing runner on the track team, a friend of one of her many prospects. But as fine as he is, I only think of David when he sells himself as a contender.

I inhale his cologne and feel uneasy—like I'm cheating the closer he scoots next to me on Nya's sofa.

"I'm gonna go to bed. I have an early and long day tomorrow."

"We don't have anything planned," Nya adds.

"I'm hitting the road."

"Already? I thought you were gonna be here for a few more days."

"That was the plan, but things change."

Nothing changed. My executive decision to leave her apartment and the track star brings me a huge relief. I'm still tied to David. The wound of leaving him is fresh. Our bond is still present. I don't want to be around any other man romantically. *My heart* and *my body* are still shackled to my rock star singing sweet words in his one-of-a-kind voice that owns me.

I ARRIVE in Rochester and rip off the Band-Aid, knowing it's a mistake. The lines of communication with David are re-opened, making the pain of leaving him fresh in my chest.

"We've got a show at the Music Farm in Charleston. Will you come? I'll pay for the flight."

"I'll try, but I can't make any promises," I say, knowing seeing him would be a mistake.

I would stay with him if I went. I'd escape the frigid temperatures of the northeast, the early landfall of snow before it's even Halloween, and forget about school to watch him live out his dream while abandoning mine. And so, I don't go.

Soon after, the flowers stop arriving, and the texts and the letters stop. The dead silence hurts like hell, and I start the healing process all over again from losing him.

25

WITHOUT YOU

DAVID

*S*even days and not a word from Maeva. Not even three dots on the bottom of our text message thread.

I text her every day for a week to tell her I love her. Eventually, she responds, suggesting we write letters like they used to do in the old days.

It'll be romantic, she writes.

I agree in a sneaky attempt to get her address. Also, because she asked me to and has never asked for much. Whatever she wants, she'll get from me.

In my letters, I do more than profess my love. I send her lyrics she inspired me to write. Have flowers sent to her every weekend. Tell her how badly I miss her. Give her updates on the band. The album. Our upcoming tour. And beg to visit.

Her reply never changes. "That's not a good idea. It was hard leaving you when I did. I don't think I can handle seeing you so soon."

"We have a gig coming up in your hometown. It'd be good if

you can make it down. Show me the hot spots. Teach me about where you're from."

"I'm so busy, David. I can't make any promises, but I'll try."

She doesn't show up or call that weekend, and I begin to grow doubt. Maybe she doesn't love me like she says. Maybe I am better off being single, being present for the ride in front of me, unclouding my head of all the misery and sorrow this split has rained upon me.

My last letter goes unanswered, and out of nowhere, the label uproots us from our southern roots into a ritzy apartment in New York City while we record our album. It's the perfect reason to reach out to Maeva, but I don't. I map out the distance between us and go stir crazy, having no time to drive upstate and surprise her due to the loaded schedule that barely allows time to sleep.

It's been six weeks since I've looked into those brown eyes, with five hours between us. Once again, I find myself beefin' with time. It refuses to play Cupid and reunite us. It occupies me with interviews instead. Photo Sessions. Rehearsals. Studio time. And appearances.

The label introduces the band to hair and makeup. They cut my hair so low I can slide my hands clean across it. I'm closely shaved with a goatee around my mouth. I look like a new man. Feel like a new man. And begin acting like a new man.

I read Maeva's note she left in our hideaway one final time.

Dear David,

Time is being unkind to us. Somehow our stars aligned knowing the wiring would get crossed. It's unfair, I know. I couldn't say this to you face to face, but this is easier if we have a clean break. I'll always be rooting for you and miss you already. I love you, David. Always.

~Maev

I ADD her note to the small stack of letters she'd written me and finally stop fighting the truth and accept her words. Clean break.

The band completes the album, and the first single charts as we prepare to hit the road, where temptation finds me damn near every night. Girls cling to us like magnets in the streets, in VIP sections at clubs, and at listening parties.

Loneliness settles in, and I surrender to the flesh of random girls whose names I never ask for, thinking of Maeva every time I strap on the rubber, wishing it was her below me, looking up at me with her sultry brown eyes, moaning my name, and waking up in my bed.

Some chick scratches my back while I'm taking my frustrations out on her in a bathroom backstage out at UPenn. I'm unkind after I get mine and ask her to leave me be for the rest of the night.

I lock the hotel door when she leaves and clean the wounds in the shower. I check out the gashes in the mirror and resent what I'm becoming, hating my reflection when my eyes stare back at me—the man Maeva predicted I'd become that would break her heart, even though she broke mine first.

I fault my mother and hers for driving her away, making her

fear what we could have been...what we are. And I refuse to accept that the last time I saw her was the end of us. That isn't and will never be my reality. We ain't over. Not by a long shot.

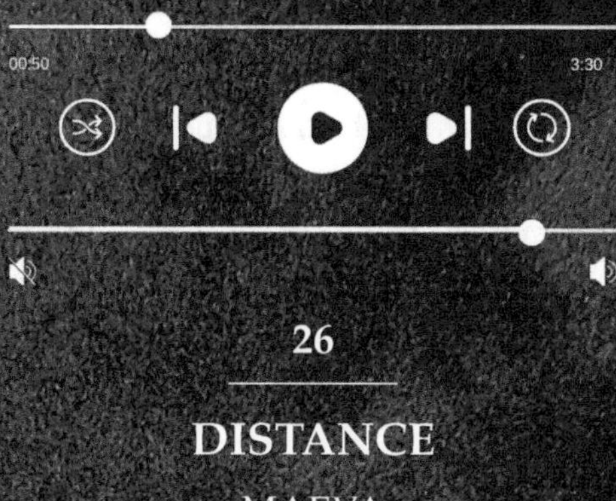

26

DISTANCE

MAEVA

Song: "Distance" by Yebba

I delve into my studies, read my texts ahead of schedule, and design pieces for portfolios before the due date. I practically live in the shop. So does Kenny, the only other student of color in my class.

Our professor pairs us together for every major assignment. I object for several reasons but keep my head down and don't rock the boat as a freshman. Outside of my objections, pairing the only two Black students in class every time, I don't complain because our contrasting styles work well together, but his looks are distracting. Six-two, medium build with biceps that flex when he lifts woodwork and benches in class, Kenny has caught the eye of every girl on campus.

They huddle about in the courtyard and whisper about him, staring at him like they're on the playground in elementary school when the cute boy walks by. If David didn't occupy my mind all the time, I'd probably join in. Funny how the heart controls the mind.

Kenny and I barely speak in class, and I keep the chatter to a minimum when we're forced to work together. I offer zero personal details about myself and change the subject when he offers up bits and pieces of his story.

"We got an A-minus on the last project. I'd like to aim for an A-plus this time," I say.

He scoffs. "And they say I'm a perfectionist."

I wrinkle my face and give him a once-over, biting my tongue to keep it civil. He pretends not to notice I'm staring at him, or that his choice of words is a dig at me, and rolls the armoire we created to the floor. I reach for the acetone and apply it to my blades.

"What are you doing with those?" he questions.

"I'm about to chisel the feet."

He scrunches his mouth. "Don't you think ball feet would look better on this beauty?"

I lower my goggles as if they're sunglasses. "I beg your pardon?"

"Ball feet will really make it stand out."

"The chiseled look will complement the ridges and hardware."

"I disagree." He lifts the leg and places a ball below it. "See?"

"Have you always been this cocky?"

"Have you always been mean?"

"I'm not mean." I sigh. "Just put the balls on. Call it compromise."

He chuckles. "This is the most spirited conversation we've had."

I put away my tools.

"I love being your partner by the way."

"Why?"

"Because you're good. It's obvious you know you are, but I never got the chance to tell you, so I'm telling you now." He smiles.

I turn my head and blush. "Thank you," I say with my back

turned to him. "You're not too far from being on my level." I face him and laugh.

Kenny's smile grows bigger. "Who would have thought you told jokes."

I fan him off. "Just put the balls on."

I reactivate quiet mode. He sneaks peeks at me as we polish our design. I look at him on the sly in return while completing my part of the finish.

"Don't let this go to your head, but your craftsmanship is impeccable, and your chip carving décor shows you have good technique. Who taught you?"

"All the credit goes to my pop."

"I'm sure he's proud of you. I would be. You have an eye for this sort of thing."

"Thank you."

"Care to grab a beer with me after this and trade stories? Perhaps become friends—maybe?"

I think about him calling me mean. "Sure," I reply with an image of David doing what I told him to do—move on.

We place our aprons on our hooks and share an appetizer and drinks in our work gear, covered in wood chips from the waist to our dusty boots. The wall has been broken down, and with ease, we discuss the pros and cons of our classes, the snow culture of the northeast, and where we see our careers in five years.

I learn Kenny is a nice guy, shy about his good looks, and less rigid outside of class.

"I'm glad we finally hung out. I've been wanting to do this with you for a while now, but I was intimidated to approach you," he admits.

"Wow. You really think I'm mean?"

"Not anymore."

The waitress returns with a second round of drinks and an

order of potato skins. We reach for the plate at the same time and giggle when our hands touch.

"It's hell living on a student budget, isn't it?" he jokes.

"Especially when you know your parents can afford to send you an extra hundred dollars but don't because they're teaching you a lesson about money." I shake my head. "This is the second time I've enjoyed a meal out. I'm sick of eating cold sandwiches and ramen when I miss the cafeteria after leaving the shop so late."

"I feel ya. I'm craving a home-cooked meal."

I raise my glass. "Here's to dorm life."

"To dorm life," he repeats after me.

I reach halfway over the table and clink his glass.

"One more time. If we don't look into each other's eyes, that's seven years of bad sex," Kenny points out.

I withdraw my mug. "That applies to making toasts."

"I'm pretty sure it applies here too." He gazes at me. "Cheers."

Our glasses clink, and I take a sip, suddenly overwhelmed by a cough as the song over the speaker catches me off guard.

"I'm cutting myself off after this one."

"Why? Can't handle your liquor? Or will your boyfriend not like you hanging out with me?"

I listen to David sing his fuckin' heart out over the track and hold back tears. "I'm not spoken for at the moment."

Kenny's voice elevates, "Ah! To be continued."

WE BUNDLE in our coats and brace ourselves for the cold walk back to the dorms. Snowflakes blow on us as we walk below the linden trees, fooling us that another round of snow is arriving faster than the news reported.

The flurries look magical in the lights from the campus lampposts and clear navy sky with a fraction of the moon peeking behind the gray clouds.

"I'm this way." I point to my hall.

"I know," he says. "I would ask for your number, but if I'm being honest, I already found it in the directory. This is me formally asking if I can use it tonight."

"And this is me not being mean. Yes, you may."

I scurry inside and keep my coat on while rocking in my study chair, listening to the last voicemail message David left me. I smell the dead rose pressed flat in my diary from the last bouquet he sent, then I type in the band's name on my web browser.

I hesitate to hit send, prolonging the torture of seeing his face. How happy he is without me. What famous model or actress is hanging on his arm. What the blogs are saying about his personal life.

My RA calls my room line. "Maeva Martin has a guest."

"I'll be right down."

I backspace the bad idea sitting in my search bar and find Kenny standing in the lobby near the frosted door.

"Yes?" I ask him.

He wraps me in his arms, tilts me backward, and kisses me with no tongue. "This is how tonight should have ended."

I'm as still as the frozen ice on the steps outside.

He lifts me up. "There's a storm coming this way. I think we should ride it out together in my room. Is that okay with you?"

27

———

FELL IN LOVE WITH A BOY

MAEVA

Song: "Fell In Love With A Boy" by Joss Stone

Kenny's dorm room is bigger than mine. His roommate never arrived, so his setup is open with the bed against the wall, plenty of walking space, and decorated with sports teams paraphernalia and car models stacked on wooden shelves he's built, reminiscent of a man cave or typical bachelor pad.

I skim his sketchbook on his dresser. "These are nice."

His lips pucker. "Coming from you, that means a lot." He glares at me. "Let me take your coat."

I sit on the sofa while he spreads wine, cheese, beer, chips, and pretzels next to a deck of cards and a Jenga box on a table in the center of his room. He joins me on the plaid couch and cues a streaming app to play a new release.

"Do they always party on your floor, or is it because of the storm?"

"I wish it was because of the storm. I don't know how anyone on that end of the hall hasn't flunked out."

"That much, huh?"

"We can check it out if you want then come back here and chill."

I shiver from a chill creeping in the room. "No thanks. I don't party much. And I don't care to be around a bunch of drunken idiots."

"Here's a blanket." Kenny unrolls a fuzzy throw from the corner of his side of the couch. "They give us just enough heat in here not to freeze in this place."

"Same in my room."

"Which game do you wanna lose first? Spades or Jenga?"

"Me...lose? Stack the Jenga blocks so I can show you how to work wood."

Kenny's eyes grow big, and the pillow in his lap shifts.

Damn, I'm going to have to watch my words.

I throw the blanket around my shoulders and drop to my knees to set up the pieces of the game. Kenny covers his erection and stalls with an awkward laugh.

"I'll go first," I say, sliding a middle piece from the center.

He counters my move and pulls out a center piece higher up. "You're gonna lose. I just want you to know that."

He follows my moves with a parallel strategy. Once I catch on to what he's doing, I make a daring move and ease a corner piece with steady hands then level the game before it topples. He studies the pieces for a long time. I get up from the floor and sit back on the couch, bouncing my legs with impatience.

While I wait for him to lose, I pour wine in a red plastic cup and sip through laughter as Kenny stalls his loss.

"Give up," I tease. "I'm unbeatable."

"That's what I get for talkin' shit." He moves his poor selection, and the pieces tumble.

I cackle. "Who's the loser again?"

"Me...in more ways than one if I don't kiss you right now." He climbs on top of me and asks, "Do I have your permission to proceed?"

"Yes."

It's been months since I've been Frenched. His tongue withdraws mine from my mouth, and they coil. I breathe heavy in his mouth, ignited from the lack of touch.

As he kisses me with the intensity of a fire blazing from the sun, his captive cock presses against me. It's so hard I cream in my panties from the friction.

Kenny stops and smiles at me with pure lust in his eyes. I stare up at him, clueless of what to say. He kisses me with his eyes open. The brown in his eyes deepens to a darker shade up close, and I play out what's about to go down in my head—or least hope it goes down that way.

Everything I remember about sex crosses my mind as he hunches on me. I pant and rock in the same rhythm as him, growing wetter from my forgotten enjoyment of humping and yearning as action builds up between us. I haven't felt this level of desire in months, and I'm responding to his advances like a harlot in heat.

"You want me to fuck you or make love to you?" Kenny asks me.

I'm too embarrassed to tell him I've already come and shy away my kisses.

He panics. "Did I say something wrong?"

"No. It's not you." I push up to slide him back off me. "We should probably talk about this first."

"I have protection, if that's what you're worried about."

"It's not, but that's good to know." I give him a kind smile. "You should know I'm in love with someone. If we do this, it might be a one-time thing. I don't know how I'm going to feel afterward. Okay?"

"Are you saying you only want something physical with me?"

I stay silent.

"That's a first. Do I put you off or something?"

"Not at all. I'm just warning you...you have a tough act to follow."

Kenny grins. "Well, let me prove you wrong."

He unsnaps the front of my bra. I jump, unaware his hands were so close to my breasts when he exposes them. He runs circles around my nipples in a delicate fashion, nibbling on them with sensual tongue play.

He sighs a groan and runs his face between them. My nani jumps in my jeans as he startles me with a swift flick of his finger that unbuttons my denim. He slides down my zipper and pulls my pants down to my boots.

"Mmm, clean up on aisle one," his voice carries as he smells my drip.

I kick off my boots. Kenny rips my jeans from around my ankles and works his way up my body, sucking on my legs until his tongue reaches my panties. He gently gnaws on my labia through my thong. The procrastination of his promising deliberation to excavate my pussy excites me to lift my ass for exploration.

He glides my panties to the side and licks my slit with a long, hard stroke. I sigh, holding onto the armrest behind me. His fingers tickle my clit while he drinks from my cup, sopping my plate like his tongue is a biscuit.

His mouth slips north. The tip of his tongue motions side to side with fast strides, withdrawing a, "*Yes,*" from me. Kenny spreads me open with his thumbs, and my back arches. My head tilts back, and I release, trembling in his mouth as he drinks from me with his lips tightly bound to my nook.

The clasp of his belt buckle rustles against his pants. The sound triggers me to lift my head. His third leg springs above his sweats, and he moves forward.

I hold him back. "Aren't you forgetting something?"

A frustrated scoff leaves his mouth. "Yeah. One sec."

I regain control of my breathing, and my heart rate slows as I watch his ass muscles retract while he searches his drawer—or pretends to. Suddenly, I feel uncomfortable. My instincts tell me to grab my clothes and go back to my room.

Kenny moves from the dresser and ransacks a box under his bed. While he's occupied, I reach for my panties from the table and slip them on. He makes his way back over to me, holding his rod in his hand.

Above me he stands. "Tell me you're prepared for moments like this."

My brows raise. "Sorry." I shake my head.

His face declines. "Fuck." He exhales then looks at me with whimpering eyes. "How 'bout you return the favor for a little bit?" He gestures, waving his dick in my face.

His isn't the microphone I want to sing into. I lean back and look up at him with enlarged eyes at his audacity. The expression on his face reads he is serious with his suggestion, and my blood begins to boil, wondering if he thinks I'm a fool.

"You can't possibly think I'm going to slob on a knob that obviously doesn't use condoms." I move around him and reach for my pants. "I'm gonna go. We can try this on another night when you're prepared for company," I say, knowing I'll never return here.

"Wait. I'll go next door and borrow some."

"Oof. That's okay." I jump to my feet, dressing as fast as I can to get out of there.

Kenny presses me to the wall and rubs his bare penis against my stomach. "Jerk me off," he whispers.

I pity him. The breathiness in his plea and the desperation in his voice moves my hand to his twitching limb. It's girthy and brown, sturdy and ready to be milked. I guide his anxious limb away from my stomach and stroke it vigorously.

Kenny rests his head on my shoulder. I wet my fingers and

massage him faster, patiently listening to him groan in my ear until he gurgles and shoots on the carpet.

He whines. "I could kick myself for not having a rubber."

I allow him to rest against me for a few seconds then layer up in my clothes.

"I thought you were going to spend the night?" He holds onto me from behind.

"I will on another night," I lie.

"At least let me walk you home."

"You don't have to. I'll be fine." I throw my bag over my shoulder.

Kenny ignores me. He throws on a sweatshirt and his coat and catches up to me in the lobby. He huddles up to me for warmth along the walk, and I'm grateful for his body heat.

I shiver on the steps in front of my building and kiss him good night. "See you tomorrow in class?"

"Yeah." He smiles. "See you there."

Aidy, my roommate, pries in my business when I walk through the door. She gives me a once-over and looks at the clock on the desk.

"I thought you finally got laid."

"You thought wrong," I answer her while washing my hands profusely.

I turn on the shower to warm our cold, unheated bathroom. "Can't Quit You" comes on the radio, and I lose it.

"Please turn that off!"

Aidy laughs. "What is it with you and that song? I like it," she says, turning down the volume. "Where you coming from?"

"You wouldn't believe me if I told you."

"Try me."

"I had drinks with Kenny."

"And you didn't go back to his place?" She throws a pencil at me. "What is wrong with you?"

"He was playing me."

"Of course he was. He has every girl on campus swooning after him."

"He didn't have one condom in his room after he said he did. Then he was all like, 'I can go get some from next door.'"

"Yikes. He was gonna go next door to brag he was getting some ass—or should I say more ass."

"Right. Major turnoff. Why would I want the boys next door in my business? I couldn't get out of there fast enough."

I cleanse the evening off in a hot shower. The snow begins to hammer down on campus, and I watch the flakes fly in the wind until it puts me to sleep. At 3 a.m., I wake up shivering and blow a condensation cloud from my mouth.

"We lost power," says Aidy, up reading a book below the covers. "The RA said it should be back on shortly."

I throw on a sweater and lay an extra blanket on my bed. "I'll ask my parents to co-sign on an apartment next year if you will."

"If it has a fireplace, you've got a deal. You think Kenny's dorm lost power too?"

I shrug below my blanket. "Probably."

"Perfect night to be snuggled up under someone."

I agree with her but don't say, wishing the body to heat me up wasn't hundreds of miles away. I put on an extra pair of socks and throw on a sweater then tremble in my cold bed, wondering if the body I yearn to lie next to me is keeping someone else warm.

28

CROSS MY MIND

MAEVA

*K*enny and I present our group project before the weekend hits. He recognizes I'm not returning his smiles and advances, and it takes less than a week for us to go back to normal and for me to see him walking hand in hand with another girl on campus.

I barge in my room to tell Aidy what I saw. She's crying on her bed, her face swollen and red.

I hold her hand and drop a tear of my own because when those I am close to cry, I cry with them.

"My grandmother passed away," she weeps hysterically.

"I'm so sorry. What can I do to help?"

She sniffles. "Let my professors know I'll be away, I guess."

"When do you leave?"

She shrugs. "Tonight, if I'm up to it."

I email Aidy's professors with the news of her bereavement and sit with her through the night. In the morning, she's a wreck. Her hands are jittery. She's sleepy and unable to drive.

"I need to hit the road, Maeva."

"I think you'll be better off taking the train."

"I don't do trains or buses. What if you drove me? You did say whatever you could do to help. I'd appreciate it."

"A death in the family is rather personal. I don't think I'll be comfortable."

"We have plenty of space. Spare rooms. My brother's apartment out back above the garage can be all yours. You can be off on your own and out of the way if that bothers you. I just need your help getting me home."

We load up her car and travel to Bridgeport, Connecticut. The occasion is sad, but deep down, I'm happy to get away from Rochester. I've been stuck in this town since I arrived, and Connecticut sounds like the perfect getaway to me.

I meet her grieving family then settle in her brother's studio —out of the way and out of the family's business.

With nothing to do, I snoop through her brother's things while the family is gathered in the main house. A few hours later, I regret not offering to drive my car and plan my escape back to school.

I power up my laptop and search for bus tickets back upstate. My search for prices and departure points reveal I'm only an hour away from New York City.

My chest pounds from learning I'm closer to David than I have been for months. I plug in the address from his last letter, tingling all over. The pounding in my chest beats stronger in my ears. I have to see him. A glimpse will do. Close up or far away, I yearn to look at him in the flesh one more time.

I type Zone 615 in the search bar and pull up the band's website. There he is, front and center on the screen. My David. He's changed, but it's him. Looking happy and mature with a new look. At peace. Sexier.

His low tapered haircut makes me swoon. The trimmed hair on his face sends me into a frenzy, and I find myself smiling at him with tears forming in my eyes. I miss him desperately and hate that it's so hard to completely let him go.

I search their name on social media, using hashtags, and scroll at fan accounts, hurting myself intentionally as I dig for pictures I know I don't want to see—can't handle seeing.

Photos of him hugged up with groupies and fans and whores fill the search. Girls that look nothing like me are cozied up to him so close they make me want to close my phone. But I continue with the self-torture and scroll down timelines of stage images, fan clicks, and behind-the-scenes snapshots.

In a matter of seconds, a cold scowl rises on my face. A picture of David at an intimate performance catches my eye. He is seated center stage, captured in his essence of crooning to the crowd, wearing a t-shirt with my face wearing his cowboy hat, blown up to cut off the rest of the image at my shoulder.

I convince Aidy's brother to drive me to the train station. I board the railway and wind up on 125th street in Harlem. Famous for its Renaissance Era in the 1920s and 1930s. Home to living legends, Black entertainers, cultural traditions, and the heart of the Civil Rights Movement.

I kill time and take in what I can after rush hour then navigate to East Houston Street by Uber. The line is long to enter the Mercury Lounge. *Zone 615* is on display in black letters above the door. Girls in t-shirts with the band's faces hold out their hands for a wrist band, outnumbering men to get inside.

I make it past the velvet rope, and déjà vu hits me. The lounge reminds me of the dive I met David in. I press my luck and test the bartender for shits and giggles. I have no problem receiving a drink, thanks to a random guy sitting next to me.

He keeps me entertained as the crowd piles in, cheering for the show to start with whistles and screams. Like a lightning bolt, I'm struck.

"New York City! Y'all ready to hear some country boys!"

His voice sends chills throughout my body. My back tenses,

and my throat stops mid swallow. My new friend at the bar pats me on my back and laughs, assuming I'm chugging too fast.

David lets out his first note. I turn toward the stage with tears in my eyes. He sings his heart out. I observe him, smiling with the guys onstage, enjoying himself in front of the crowd, doing what he loves, and standing where he belongs.

The spectators surrounding me watch the band in amazement. I am too, singing every few words between crying spells. Emotion fills my body. I wipe away my proud tears, hiding them before I'm labeled crazy by strangers.

I look around to see if anyone has noticed. All I see is a room full of people loving on the love of my life—something I could never compete with.

The crowd amps up when they hear notes from "Bittersweet Symphony." I sway along with the horde while contemplating my next move. Do I make my way backstage? Do I stand under a light so he can see me? Or do I leave now that I've done what I set out to do? I've seen him. I've heard his amazing voice. But my feet refuse to move to the exit.

I check the time and begin to count the minutes before I have to leave and catch the last train out of Harlem back to Bridgeport.

David goes into transition. "New York! We wanna play something for you we've been working on. This song holds a special place in my heart. I hope you like our rendition of this classic."

I take one final look at him shine on stage and turn to leave.

David's raspy, magnetic voice sings, "Baby, let's cruise."

My shoulders sink, and my knees weaken. My body turns to face him on its own, and I stand locked in place as he croons Smokey Robinson's hit. Women all around me shout his name through the final note. The crowd goes wild, and they crank up the venue with the single I have avoided listening to like the plague.

As they close out the evening, skank-clad girls rush past me to exit the club. They head to the side of the building where the bus is waiting for the band. I follow them, blending in with the groupies, then I break away to the brick wall of the next building when the pandemonium of screaming and pushing fans erupts.

The band is headed for the bus. Security bum-rushes the crowd and forms a path. I get a closer look of Lim, Souse, Moe, and David—now superstars, signing t-shirts, boobs, and flyers, and posing for pictures.

Their road manager scurries them to safety, and I take my final look at my old flame then leave the alley to wait for my ordered car under the flashing white lights at the front entrance of the club. When it arrives, I text David:

That was absolutely beautiful.
I'm so proud of you.

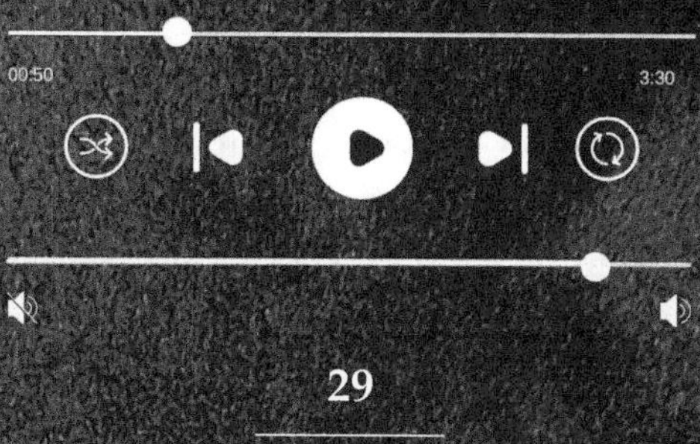

29

CAN'T QUIT YOU

DAVID

"Can't Quit You" by T.K. Richards

The rush is everything I imagined. Playing in front of a packed house is unbelievable, and the shows are *bouta* get larger. They say if you can make it here, you can make it anywhere, and I view the reception of this New York crowd as a tell-tale sign that we have arrived.

A couple standing at the foot of the stage sing along when they aren't kissing one another. The hoots and hollers fuel my empty tank with the energy I need from the late nights spent in the studio and the ripping and running that's slowly wearing me down. But I'm not the only one on a high, judging by the celebratory smiles on the guys' faces as we bring down the house.

This used to be a vision in my dreams, and it's now come to life. Zone 615 has made it. Local country boys are now a household name with fans traveling from city to city to hear us play. May this buzz be everlasting.

Girls pull on me, place their panties in my pockets, beg for kisses and pictures and autographs. It's flattering, overwhelming, annoying, and strange.

Post this show, the mania feels heightened. Our fanbase has grown, and safety is now an issue. So much so that security has to escort us to the bus.

Our road manager, Toad, instructs us, "Three minutes and that's it. Sign as you walk. No lingering for people wanting selfies. Let's keep it moving and board the bus, fellas."

We fancy as many requests time allows. Take quick pics. Sign posters, printed articles, and tickets from the show. So many eyes are upon me, distant and up close. Empty eyes. Drunk eyes. Dark eyes. Hungry eyes.

The hair on my neck rises as my name is called from every angle. That overwhelming feeling begins to sink in, and I scurry to the bus.

A cross between being adored by music lovers and being stalked by fanatics worries me as I'm unable to tell the difference at times. I exhale from a sense of feeling safe once I wave to the crowd from the steps of the bus and disappear to my section in the back. The boys all board moments later, and like always, we huddle and give thanks to the man upstairs for a good show.

While we wait for the party to clear so we can leave the lot, Toad shares a word.

"David, you sounded great out there tonight. Rest up those vocals." His brows curve. "We picked up two more shows next week while you boys were performing."

Lim asks, "Whoever did the sound needs to come on the road with us. Any way of poaching him?"

"I'll see what I can do."

I open my mouth to second that when I hear Souse and Moe whispering Maeva's name. "What'd you say?"

Moe looks away and holds his response.

"Why are you two talking about Maeva?"

Souse shakes his head. "I think I saw her tonight."

"Where? When?"

He points to the front. "Out there when we were getting on the bus."

I shoot past him. "Why didn't you say anything?"

"It was dark. I'm a little tipsy. And I'm not a hundred percent sure."

Toad shouts, "Don't get off this bus!"

Moe adds, "It could have been someone who favors her, beau. There are a lot of pretty girls out there."

"And none of them compare to her."

Scattered screams erupt from the dispersed crowd when I search for her through the big window on the front of the bus. Maeva's face isn't among them. I run back to my section and dig through my bag for my phone. My garments fall on the floor as I empty it to reach the muffled buzzing lost in the shuffle.

The screen is lit with a message from Maeva. I open it, and my world spins. I waste not another second to dial her number.

"Please pick up. Please pick up," I mumble below my breath.

"Hey." Her voice deflates me.

"Baby, tell me you're outside."

"I'm in a cab on my way to Harlem. The last train leaves soon."

"Tell 'em to turn around."

"But I'll miss my—"

"Maev, let me worry about how you get home. Please turn around."

My chest pounds louder than Moe's drums on stage when she asks the driver to bring her back to the club. I can hear her smiling through the phone.

"I'll be there in a minute."

"Meet me out front." I hang up and yell to Toad. "I've gotta get off this bus."

Toad orders the driver to pull out of the lot and park on the main street. I throw on a baseball cap and my coat, wrap a scarf around me that my mother knitted to cover the lower half of my face, and sneak past the leftover stans in the alley.

A pale-blue Chevy veers toward the club entrance, and butterflies swarm in the pit of my stomach. Her hair is the first thing I see rising from the backseat. Still wild. Still beautiful.

I pay the driver a tip through the passenger window. He skirts off, and I face my love standing too far away from me.

"Baby, come here." I pick her up by her waist and swing her around.

Her floral perfume surrounds us when I place her on her feet. Maeva giggles as my cold hands slide across her warm cheeks.

"I'm never letting you go again." I take in her scent, close my eyes, and kiss the softest lips I've struggled to live without.

The lights on the sign with the band's name flicker above us. The clicking sound breaks our coiling tongues, and we look up.

"Zone 615 has their name in lights," she says.

Our eyes meet, and I gaze into hers below the blinking. The brown hues in her eyes are highlighted by the flashing lights with gold specks, and her skin glistens like champagne diamonds in the night.

"Come on." I escort her to the bus.

Toad introduces himself, and Maeva waves to the band.

I nod to the driver. "Get us home as fast as you can."

Moe hops out of his seat. "You and I are better than a hand-shake." He hugs her a little too close for my taste. "It's good to see you."

"It's good to see all of you," she says. "Congratulations."

I take her to the back of the bus and close the door behind me. We stare at each other on mute with smiles on both of our faces until she kills the silence.

"Hey, Smokey." She brushes against me. ""Cruisin"?"

I chuckle. "I can't believe you're in front of me right now." I kiss her. "Maev, I miss you. And I've never stopped loving you."

Her hand touches my face, and I fall to pieces. "Well, I'm here, so what does that tell you?"

We skip the grand tour of the house and run to my room. Maeva wants me to jump her bones right away, and I couldn't be happier knowing she's missed my touch as much as I've missed hers. She strips away her coat and hat. I join her in the race to get naked, pulling off my coat and shirt with one move, and trip while pulling off my jeans, hopping on one leg to get next to her.

Impassioned kisses consume us. We lock lips and lose our balance as my fingers spark when they touch her topless body. We fall on my bed, exchanging breathy sighs. I hold her in my arms, slowing down the inevitable to taste her tongue—a flavor I've held on to since the day I last saw her.

She spreads her legs below me and pulls as I push, kissing me with perfection. Slow and tender.

My hands roam her body, pausing on her breasts. I cup each nipple in my mouth then bite them precisely on the tip.

She squirms and releases a sigh above my head. "Ah." Her moans sing like music to my ears.

I toggle between each brown splendor.

"Stop torturing me," she whines.

I grin at her anxious nature and draw a line down her torso with my chin. She splays her southern lips with her fingers. I nibble on each limb, making her fidget, for she knows what's coming.

I taste her saccharine nectar formed on the cusp. Her back stiffens, and her legs relax when I lick her throbbing pussy into submission. My finger slides in, and she expels gratification through obscenities she's never voiced before then whispers below her hitched breath.

"Stand up."

I do as she commands. She rolls to the edge of the bed and delivers the smoothest kiss to my cock. I tremble from her power.

Her luscious, sultry suction. The entirety of her mouth swallows me, and I bloom in season, fully swollen on her tongue.

"I've gotta have you right now." I groan and pull out.

I mount her, lifting her legs high and wide. My pipe drives inside her lines relentlessly. My thigh muscles tighten then quiver from initial impact. Maeva squeezes her walls, and I twizzle myself loose, digging out the drip I secretly cried for some nights.

She moans and cries for me while I drill her tenderness with deliberate concentration for her pleasure, losing myself in the contractions of her wet flesh. Her panting incites a riot within me. She feels too good to make love to in this moment. Her warmth and wetness compel me to fuck her senseless. I can feel she wants that. Needs it. Craves it.

Selfishly I stroke her harder, faster and deeper, unable to hold back my built-up aggression. I dip into every corner, every inch, every ridge of her cave. She pants as I strike her white gold with the speed and agility of a sailor gone out at sea for too long, finally home to make up for lost time.

My neck shifts my head from studying Maeva's orgasmic expression of her teeth biting her bottom lip to the gold sculpture of a guitar on the wall above her.

I explode inside of her gloriousness. "Good God!"

Maeva's pussy pulsates with me locked deep inside, grunting and squeezing me dry. My shoulders shiver before I flop on top of her.

"Maeva, baby." I kiss her supple mounds and her neck until I reach her sinuous lips. "Hey," I say into her mouth.

"Hey, you." Her eyes *smize* into mine.

I trace her cheeks then her lips with my finger, continuing my caress down to her folds. I strum her clit like my guitar, stimulating her one more time so I can hear her sensuous moans trickle from her lips.

"Don't stop," she orders, biting her knuckle.

"Your every wish is my command."

Her legs tighten and lay straight as her back locks in an arch. "Oh, ah, iy." She shivers and sighs, grabs my hand, and holds it in place.

I kiss her glorious body from head to toe until she falls asleep where she belongs—in my arms.

Light shades of gray slip through the drapes when she wakes. I've been up watching her sleep for an hour, unable to wipe away the smile she puts on my face.

"Maev, can we have a conversation about how this can work?"

She grunts and nestles in my arms. "Is a conversation really necessary?"

I look down at her. "What are you saying?"

She kisses my chest. "I want you, David."

I lift her on top of me and smile. "It's about damn time."

REVIEWS ENCOURAGE VORACIOUS INTEREST EVERY WHERE TO SUPPORT

ME, THE AUTHOR

I GREATLY APPRECIATE IT

XOXO

ALSO BY T.K. RICHARDS

Thank you for diving into my fictional worlds. Let's stay in touch.
Sign up for newsletter at the link below.
https://tkrichardsnewsletter.ck.page

T.K. RICHARDS is a multi-genre author with popular novels and novellas in several genres of romance including Black, Inter-racial/Multicultural & Paranormal Romance, Speculative Fiction, Women's Fiction, and Domestic Thrillers. A graduate of Lime-stone University, T.K. has honors in Expository Writing, and was also the Poet Laureate of her graduating class. When she is not writing, she is immersed in the world of tennis, and binge watching movies—mostly comedy as she loves to laugh.

For more information about **T.K. Richards**, visit her website at www.tkrichards.com and subscribe to her newsletter at: https://tkrichardsnewsletter.ck.page

Playlist for Can't Quit You on Spotify: https://open.spotify.com/playlist/5CDUsnSYBjgQAıRgXXDHmB?si=jVHjV-VuQrKuıvMhyudt6w&pi=u-b5FiMhzdTEym

Follow T.K. RICHARDS on the platforms listed below to interact with her personally:

tkrichards.substack.com

pinterest.com/TKWrites

tiktok.com/@tkrwrites

youtube.com/tkrichards

amazon.com/author/Tkrichards

goodreads.com/T.k.richards

bookbub.com/authors/t-k-richards

patreon.com/tkrichards

instagram.com/t.k.richards

bsky.app/profile/tkrichards

00:50 3:30

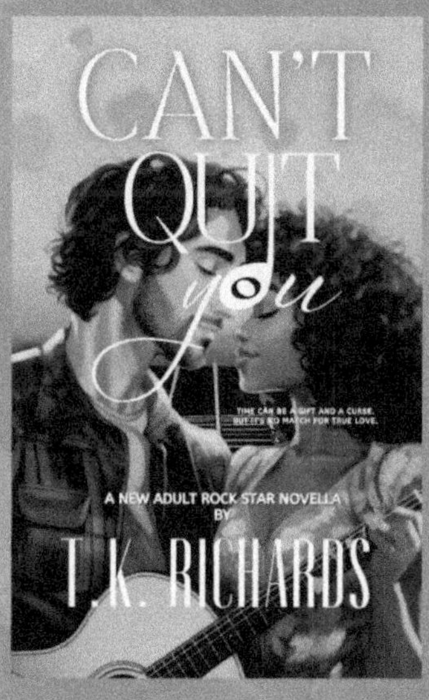
CAN'T QUIT you
TIME CAN BE A GIFT AND A CURSE.
BUT IT'S NO MATCH FOR TRUE LOVE.
A NEW ADULT ROCK STAR NOVELLA
BY
T.K. RICHARDS

TIME CAN BE A GIFT & A CURSE
BUT IT'S NO MATCH FOR TRUE LOVE
CAN'T QUIT You
AN INSTALOVE NEW ADULT ROCKSTAR ROMANCE
T.K. RICHARDS